DARK RIDE

P.G. KASSEL

STORYTELLER WORKS

Print Version

ISBN 13: 978-0-9967919-2-2

Library of Congress Control

Number: 2017913898

Storyteller Works, Los Angeles, CA

Cover Design by Damonza

To the memory of Rod Serling, the master of this style of storytelling.

CHAPTER ONE
LARKIN

Officer Jack Larkin observed the witness, a junior at Reynolds High School and a part time clerk at a strip mall convenience store.

"He can't see me, right?" The clerk shuffled nervously as he peered through the one-way mirror into the interrogation room.

"He can't see you," the sergeant assured him. "Is that the man who robbed you this morning?"

The clerk shuffled some more, brushing his fingertips over the nasty bruise that covered most of the right side of his face.

"That bothering you?" the sergeant asked. "We can get you some aspirin."

"Nah, nah, it's okay."

"At what point did that happen?" the sergeant asked.

"The guy, the robber, grabbed me, grabbed the back of my neck and slammed my head down on the counter," the clerk answered.

"I understand that, son. I remember you telling me. But when? I mean, at what point during the robbery?"

"Sorry. Just after I opened the cash drawer. You know, to give him change for the gum. He reached across the counter."

"How long do I have to hang around here?" Marty Wedlow shouted from the interrogation room, his voice crackling through the intercom speaker.

Larkin's partner, Oscar Romero, stepped into view on the other side of the glass.

"It shouldn't be much longer, Mr. Wedlow," Romero said. "We appreciate you coming in."

"You guys just don't get that I've got stuff to do," Wedlow said.

"You just have to tell us the truth, son," the sergeant encouraged the clerk. "There's no right or wrong answer here."

"It's kinda hard to tell," the clerk said. "He was wearing a hoodie, ya know?" I mean, he's about the same size of the guy. You know, kinda thin."

"What about his face, maybe his hair color?" the sergeant pushed.

"Well, like I told ya, he had the hoodie pulled up. I'm sorry, man," the clerk said.

"So, you didn't see his face?" the sergeant tried again.

The clerk shook his head. "I'm sorry. I was, I was kinda scared."

The sergeant took a deep breath. "Okay, no problem. We appreciate you coming in." He turned to the young officer waiting next to the door. "Show him out, please."

The officer opened the door and ushered the clerk into the hallway.

"Son of a bitch!" Larkin cursed as the door closed.

"Wedlow didn't have the cash on him when you picked him up and the clerk can't make a positive ID. We can't hold him," the sergeant said.

"You think it was just a big coincidence we came across him just three blocks from that store?" Larkin snapped.

"Hey, I'm on your side," the sergeant responded.

"Yeah, yeah, I'm sorry. It's just that the slippery little ferret's done it again."

"You think maybe Wedlow had somebody working with him? Somebody he could've handed off the cash to?"

"The clerk didn't see anybody else," Larkin answered. "He was sure as hell alone when we picked him up. I thought we had a good shot at the clerk nailing him."

"Can't blame the clerk. He got himself a big enough scare to wet his pants," the sergeant said.

The door opened and Romero stepped back into the room. He pointed through the glass at Wedlow. "So, where are we?"

"Cutting him loose," Larkin said, unable to hide his anger.

"What is it with this punk and you?" Romero asked Larkin.

You haven't been here that long," the sergeant answered. "Marty Wedlow's been kicking around our fair city for some five years now. Larkin's brought him in a dozen times on a variety of charges, but he always walks away."

"He's either a mastermind criminal or the luckiest bastard that ever took a breath," Larkin answered. "And believe me, I know he's no mastermind."

"Hey, Officer Larkin," Wedlow called, grinning up at the observation glass. "I'm kinda thirsty. How about a beer?"

"It's a pain in the ass to see a guy like this get away with it all the time, but why are you so bent out of shape?" Romero asked. "This one was just a convenience store, and what did the clerk say was stolen, a hundred and twenty-nine bucks? It's small potatoes."

"This time," Larkin answered.

The sergeant picked up the manila folder from the counter beneath the observation glass. Flipping it open, he read, "Marty Wedlow, thirty-three years old. Suspicion three counts of burglary, suspicion two counts robbery. This one makes it three counts robbery — unofficially, of course."

"Still sounds like mostly small potatoes," Romero remarked.

"He talks smooth enough, but it all covers up a mean streak," Larkin advised.

"Yeah? Romero said.

"He's got multiple suspicion of assault counts in his packet," the sergeant continued reading. "Slipped the noose on all of them."

"But how?" Romero asked.

"He's got a knack," the sergeant sighed, glancing at the file. "One of them was on an elderly couple returning home from dinner one night. The assailant slipped into their garage after they pulled in, roughed up the old folks, and stole their BMW. A patrol car found the BMW the next day twenty miles away."

"Wedlow was seen in the neighborhood an hour before the attack and I picked him up within a few blocks of the stolen car," Larkin explained. "But there was no physical evidence in the vehicle and the couple said the assailant wore a mask."

"So, he's a tough guy when a victim has no way to defend themselves," Romero remarked.

"Or when they're too young or weak," Larkin added. "He's been connected to a nasty rape, a couple of burglaries, some rough snatch and grabs; he dabbles in just about anything that doesn't take a lot of thought or planning."

"Hey, Larkin, where's that beer?" Wedlow called out again.

"Looking at him, you'd never guess he had it in him," Romero said.

"He's got it in him," Larkin said.

"Maybe turning him loose is a blessing in disguise," the sergeant said. "Once he's out on the street again, it's just a matter of time. He's bound to slip up somewhere. Keep a close eye on him. Maybe the next time you bring him in it'll be for something that we can put him away for so long he won't have that arrogant grin on his face by the time he gets out."

"Yeah, well, we've wasted enough time on him today," Larkin groused.

"Yeah, get him out of here," the sergeant said.

<<< >>>

"Sure hate to see you guys waste all this time," Wedlow remarked as Larkin and Romero escorted him down the hallway.

"You never get tired of flappin' that mouth, do you?" Larkin responded.

"Just seems like every time you drag me in here, you never have any evidence. That seems like a waste of time to me. Must be just bad luck, huh?" Wedlow gibed.

"You agreed to come in with us, remember? And luck, well, it's a funny thing. Eventually the odds always turn," Larkin said.

"You talk like I've been doing something wrong," Wedlow said as they reached the booking counter.

Larkin suddenly grabbed Wedlow's arm and shoved him up against the plexiglass.

"Jack," Romero cautioned.

"You know what you've been doing, you piece of scum. And God sure as hell knows it," Larkin hissed.

"God?" Wedlow repeated. "You religious, Larkin?"

"God, the universe, fate, whatever the greater power might be," Larkin answered. "But if it is God, then there's heaven, and if there's heaven, then there's gotta be hell. And if there's hell, well, then you've got a shitload of trouble coming your way."

"Let me go, man," Wedlow said, his voice uneven.

Larkin let him go and turned to see the officer managing the front counter, watching him with some concern.

"Just a little misunderstanding," Larkin shrugged.

"I didn't see a thing," the officer muttered, turning his attention to a pile of reports in front of him.

Larkin heard the entrance doors open and turned to see two young cops he knew escorting a tall, slender man into the building. His hands were cuffed behind him. One cop carried an old fashioned, well-worn leather satchel that had to belong to their prisoner.

The man's features were rather hawkish, with a thin nose and pointed chin. He had a pallid complexion and strands of long, wiry hair fell across his prominent forehead. An old dark coat, a good century out of style, reached down below his knees.

Larkin judged the guy to be in his mid thirties, but there was something about him. He seemed much older.

"What's going on with that coat?" Wedlow chuckled. "It must be at least eighty degrees outside."

"Shut up, Marty," Larkin ordered.

"What've you got here?" Larkin asked as the cops brought the cuffed man to a stop beside the desk.

"He was putting on quite a show on a corner a couple of blocks from the beach," one cop answered. "Tarot cards, telling fortunes, predicting the future, that kind of stuff, and all of it without a street performance permit."

"Come on, Larkin," Wedlow pushed. "Let me get out of here and then you can talk with your buddies all you like."

"That his gear?" Romero asked, ignoring Wedlow and pointing at the satchel.

"Yeah," the cop answered. "All the tools of the trade."

"What'd you bring him in for?" Larkin asked.

"A couple of local business owners complained. He's not carrying any ID, and he won't tell us his name," the second cop answered.

"Yeah, why won't you tell them your name?" Larkin asked the man.

The hawkish man turned his head to look at Larkin and smiled a strange smile.

"It's not yet time," he answered, his voice old.

"What the hell does that mean?" Romero laughed.

Marty Wedlow let out a shriek. "Get it off me, get it off," he cried.

Larkin turned to see an average sized house spider crawling up Wedlow's arm to his shoulder. He leaned over and swatted it away. The spider fell to the floor and Wedlow hastily backed away from it.

"Look at this, Romero, our tough guy scared of a little spider," Larkin laughed.

The spider began moving towards Wedlow.

"I hate the damn things," Wedlow puled, backing away.

"Don't worry, Marty. I'll save you," the hawkish man said, his tone mocking.

The man stepped forward and brought his foot down on the spider.

"You know this guy?" Larkin asked the hawkish man.

"Marty? Oh, he's very well known," he replied.

There it was again, that hollow, mocking tone. Larkin felt an involuntary shudder run down his spine.

"I've never laid eyes on this guy in my life," Marty said, glaring at the hawkish man. "And what the hell, you making fun of me? So what if I can't stand spiders? Everybody's got something they're afraid of."

"And you have more than your share," the hawkish man said.

"Screw you," Marty snapped.

The hawkish man just smiled again, that thin little smile.

"Can I get out of here now?" Wedlow asked Larkin.

"The sooner the better," Larkin told him.

Wedlow took a few steps towards the door, but then spun back towards the hawkish man.

"Careful," Larkin cautioned him.

"You think you're so damn smart," Wedlow hissed at the hawkish man. "Predicting the future, my ass! Did you predict getting dragged in here today?"

The hawkish man's lips curled up in that odd smile again.

"Come on," Wedlow persisted. "How about you tell me my future? Right now."

"I agree with the officer here," the hawkish man answered, nodding at Larkin. "Yes, you might say the fates have turned against you, Marty. Your luck is changing and your time is running out."

Larkin couldn't hide his surprise. How did this guy know what he'd said to Wedlow back in the hallway? The guy wasn't even in the building at the time.

Wedlow looked a little rattled.

"All right," the first cop said. "Enough chitchat. Let's go."

He and his partner escorted the hawkish man to the booking desk.

Larkin took hold of Wedlow's arm. "Out you go, Wedlow."

"Take it easy," Wedlow responded without resisting.

Larkin marched him out the front door and onto the sidewalk.

"I know I'll see you again soon," Larkin said.

"Whatever you say," Wedlow shrugged.

Larkin watched him amble off down the sidewalk and was about to go back inside when one of the senior detectives he knew called out to him. He took a couple of minutes to catch up with the detective and then headed back inside.

"What kept you?" Romero asked.

"Just talking to a guy I know," Larkin answered.

The two cops who had brought in the hawkish man were still at the desk, completing their paperwork. He hurried over to them.

"Hey, where'd you put your guy?" Larkin asked.

"Interrogation Two," one of them responded. "Soon as we're done here we're gonna see if the sergeant can get a name out of him."

"I've got a couple of questions for him myself, if you guys don't mind," Larkin said.

"Knock yourself out."

Larkin headed down the hall with Romero behind him.

He reached the room and opened the door.

"Hey," he heard Romero blurt out behind him.

The room was empty.

CHAPTER TWO
STEVIE

Marty Wedlow walked along the city street with his usual overconfident swagger. He hated he wasn't all that strong or all that tough, but he did a pretty good job of disguising that with his walk and his attitude. Most of the time, it didn't even occur to him he was masking anything, but today it all felt like smoke and mirrors. He didn't feel confident. He felt pissed.

It pissed him off Larkin didn't even offer to give him a ride back to where they picked him up, even after he went along willingly when they asked if he'd mind going to the station to answer some questions. Of course, cooperating with the cops was all smoke and mirrors, too. And it pissed him off he had to walk over two miles to get back to where he'd left his car.

And then there was that freak he'd run up against in the police station. What'd that asshat know, anyway? He was about as real a fortune teller as a department store Santa Claus. The freak was just full of bullshit and that was all there was to it.

He dealt with his upset by visualizing the fortune teller giving him crap and then decking him with a fast right hook. He sure couldn't predict that coming. That's what he wished he could've done, but it was never like that for him. In high school, he still remembered the getting pushed around, the bullying, the humiliation.

Walking down the street, he trusted nothing. He trusted no one.

People he passed could have it out for him or mark him as somebody to screw over. He'd never met a cop who didn't want to make his life miserable.

The afternoon was hot and the sun beat down through his short, cropped hair. The ocean was less than two miles away, but today there was no cooling breeze blowing inland. He swiped his arm across his forehead to stop the sweat from dripping into his eyes. He was only a few minutes from his car, but his feet hurt. Everything was just a big pain in the ass today.

He turned the corner onto West Sixth Avenue and saw his car, a Honda Civic, in the middle of the block, right where he'd parked it. It was eight years old when he'd chiseled a guy out of it about a year earlier. The paint was in kind of terrible shape and there were a few dents, but the car ran great.

Marty pulled the car keys from his pocket as he approached the Civic. He unlocked the car and pulled the door open. And that's when he saw Stevie, fast asleep, curled up in the back seat. His longish blonde hair had fallen across one eye.

"Stevie," Marty barked.

Stevie woke, a look of fright flashing across his face. Seeing Marty, he soon recovered.

"Marty, hey. I was wondering if they'd let you go."

Marty reached down, tugged the release lever, and pulled the seat back forward.

"'Course they let me go," Marty responded as Stevie climbed out of the back. "They had nothing to stick me with."

"Yeah, yeah, right, good," Stevie said, wiping his eyes.

"What the hell were you doing, sleeping in the back of the car on a day like this?" Marty asked. "Even with those windows cracked, you were getting broiled in there."

"Yeah, it's hot. Guess I didn't notice it much once I fell asleep," Stevie said.

"Shit, you're sweating like a pig," Marty observed.

"Sorry, Marty."

"So hand over the money," Marty ordered.

Stevie dropped his eyes and shuffled nervously.

"What're you waiting for?" Marty asked.

Stevie reached into his back pocket, withdrew a wad of bills, and put them into Marty's outstretched hand. It took Marty a millisecond to count it.

"Forty-two bucks. There's forty-two bucks here," Marty said.

"Yeah," Stevie said, taking a cautious step backwards.

"Where's the rest of it?"

Stevie stared at him, nervous and scared.

"Where's the rest of it?" Marty repeated, louder than before.

"I ran into a guy I know while I was waiting for you this morning," Stevie explained.

"A guy you know," Marty repeated.

"Yeah, we've done some business before, and I really needed some help. And, well, he had a great price on—"

"You spent our money on pills?" Marty interrupted.

"I had to get some, Marty. I had to."

Marty leaped forward, took hold of Stevie, and slammed him hard against the side of the Civic. Stevie was as thin as a pencil, so it didn't take much effort.

"Your dealer has all my money now?" Marty shouted. "You spent the rest of my money on your stinking habit?"

"Please don't hit me again," Stevie pleaded, cowering against the car.

With disgust, Marty let go of him and shoved him away.

"I didn't hit you, you idiot," Marty told him.

Marty paced in front of the Civic while Stevie watched him, frightened that Marty might explode again.

"I'm sorry," Stevie said. "I'm so sorry."

"Yeah."

"It was a crappy thing to do," Stevie continued. "You trusted me with the cash, and you don't deserve what I did."

"I sure as hell didn't," Marty said. "You know I need to get out of here. You know I need to get up north. How am I supposed to do that without money? "

"No, you're right. Ever since I got into town two months ago, you let me hang with you. You've looked out for me. You didn't deserve it, man."

"Shit, Stevie, those dexies are gonna kill you if you keep at it like you are," Marty said, feeling himself calm down a little.

"Yeah."

"And how in hell did you fall asleep in the car if you were dropping those things?"

"I only took a couple," Stevie answered.

"Shit," Marty kicked the Civic's front tire. "Forty-two bucks isn't gonna help me one damn bit. I'm gonna have to find something else, and soon."

"You know I'll help you with whatever you say," Stevie said.

"Damn right you will, but not today," Marty said. "All I want to do now is get a beer and then get some sleep. Tomorrow I'll come up with something."

Marty slid behind the wheel of the Civic and slammed the door shut. Stevie approached and stood beside the driver's side window.

"Where you going now, Marty?"

"I told you. I'm going back to my room to get some rest."

"Can I come along?" Stevie asked. "I got nowhere else to hang out right now."

"Yeah, sure. But you're gonna have to sneak past the desk clerk."

"Thanks, man. Thanks."

"Just hurry up and get your ass in the car," Marty said. "I want to get unconscious before this damn day gets any worse."

CHAPTER THREE
THE MOM-AND-POP JOB

Marty found himself in a better mood after a good night's sleep. He turned the Civic onto Ashford Avenue, drove most of the way down the block and then pulled over to the curb a hundred feet short of the corner.

"You gonna kill the engine?" Stevie asked from the passenger seat.

"Not now," Marty answered.

"So, what're we doing?"

Marty pointed across the street at the neighborhood mom-and-pop grocery store one door down from the corner. The old, wooden sign above the storefront, its green lettering cracked and faded, read 'Ashford Grocery.'

"I wanted to check this out."

"The grocery store?"

"A grocery store where there's usually just one old geezer inside and a lot of ad posters blocking the front window," he answered.

"We're gonna hit it?" Stevie asked.

"I'm thinking about it."

"There won't be much money in there, a place like that," Stevie said.

"It's a little after 10:00 now," Marty said. "The place gets a lot of business early. People coming in for breakfast stuff, people stopping in on their way to work for stuff. Yeah, there's not gonna be a fortune, but since you blew through all our money, I don't have a lot of options here."

"I'm really sorry."

"Not as sorry as you're gonna be if you ever steal from me again," he told him. "I told you fifty times I need to head north and I need the cash.

"Why do you have to leave?" Stevie inquired. "I mean, you never said."

"I just need to, that's all."

Stevie remained quiet for several seconds. "Maybe I could go with you?" he said, his voice hopeful.

"Maybe."

"I wouldn't be any trouble and I'd earn my way," Stevie said.

"Yeah, maybe, I said," Marty answered. "But right now it's about the cash. That's all we're gonna do today. Look for cash."

They sat in silence for several minutes, watching the grocery store. A young mother pushing her toddler in a stroller came around the corner and went into the store. Five minutes later, she came out with a plastic grocery bag hanging from the stroller handlebar and disappeared in the direction she had come.

"I still can remember my mom pushing me around in a stroller like that," Stevie said.

"Good for you."

"What about your folks?" Stevie asked.

"What about them?"

"They still around?"

"They live in Delaware," he answered.

"You're from Delaware?"

"My dad owns a manufacturing plant there."

"What's he make?"

"Precision splines and gears for the nautical industry," he explained.

"Nautical industry?" Stevie looked baffled.

"Boats and ships," he explained. "The old man lives high off Navy contracts."

Stevie pondered the information, looking more confused with each passing second.

"So, how come you're out here?" Stevie asked.

"What do you mean?

"You know. Couldn't you be doing pretty well working with your dad?

"That was his plan," he answered.

Stevie began formulating another question, but Marty put the car into gear and pulled away from the curb.

"The place won't start getting busy again for another thirty or forty minutes," he said.

"We gonna do it?" Stevie asked.

"Yeah."

Marty made a left at the corner, drove halfway down the block, and found a parking space. Reaching into his pocket, he pulled out a switchblade, opened the glove compartment, slipped the knife inside, and closed the compartment.

"Aren't you gonna need that?" Stevie asked.

"There's a big difference between robbery and armed robbery," Marty answered. "I never carry. Anyway, I told you there's just the old guy running the store. He's not gonna be a problem."

They got out of the car, Marty locked it and then led the way back towards the grocery store. Just short of the corner, they crossed the street. Marty kept an eye on Stevie. He always expected the guy to get nervous about this kind of thing, but he never did. Stevie just walked a little behind him like a faithful dog.

They rounded the corner and strolled into the store. The old guy was behind the front counter sitting on a bar stool with worn cushions on the seat and backrest. Marty thought the guy must be at least seventy-five.

"Good morning," the old man greeted them.

"Morning. Where's your orange juice?" Marty replied.

"Refrigerator case at the back," the old man pointed.

"Thanks."

Marty took his time heading towards the back of the store with Stevie tagging behind him. Reaching the back aisle, Marty strolled from one end to the other, glancing down each of the aisles leading to the front. The store was empty.

They started back towards the front of the store. Marty grabbed a Batman comic book from the shelf and thrust it into Stevie's hand.

"Lean in the doorway and keep watch," Marty instructed, leaning in close to him. "Look like you're reading your comic."

Stevie nodded.

The old man looked up as they approached the front of the store. He looked a little puzzled.

"Couldn't find the orange...?" the old man began, trailing off when he saw Stevie walking towards the door holding the comic.

"You haven't paid for that," the old man called to him, sliding off the bar stool.

"Don't worry about him," Marty growled.

Marty reached the end of the counter and hurried around it.

"You can't come back here," the old man said, his voice cracking.

Marty smashed his open palm into the old man's chest, sending him stumbling backwards into an old cigarette rack. A dozen cigarette packs tumbled to the floor as the old man grappled for something to keep him on his feet.

He had no sooner steadied himself when Marty grabbed his arm and jerked him over to the cash register that looked like a leftover from the late sixties.

"Open it," Marty ordered, anger in his voice.

The old man keyed the register until a bell jingled and the drawer slid open. Marty shoved the old guy hard again, and he banged hard into the storage shelf set into the wall, again staying on his feet.

Marty cleaned all the bills from the drawer tray and then lifted the tray to look beneath it. Lying at the bottom of the drawer among a mess of register receipts were four plastic cards. He snatched them up, thinking he'd scored some credit cards. But looking closer, he realized they were no such thing.

"What the hell is this?" he waved the cards at the old guy.

"Gift cards for Oceanside Park," the old man answered, his voice heavy with fear. "For my son and his family."

"Shit," Marty cursed, shoving the cards into his back pocket.

"Leave them, please," the old man pleaded. "They're for my grand-children."

"Where's your safe?" Marty asked, his voice angrier and more impatient.

The old man pointed feebly to the floor in the corner.

Marty changed his position and saw a small floor space.

"Open it," he ordered.

"There's nothing in it," the old man assured him.

Marty took hold of the old guy and threw him into the corner. He cried out as he hit the wall and fell to the floor on top of the safe.

Stevie leaned back into the store to see what was happening.

"I said open it," Marty snapped.

The old man struggled to his knees and opened the metal floor plate exposing the safe dial. He dialed in the combination, took hold of the latch, and pulled open the safe.

Marty leaned over him and peered into the small container. It was empty.

"Where's the money?" Marty asked, feeling pissed.

"No reason to put any in yet today," the old man wheezed. "Not enough business."

"Son of a bitch," Marty cursed.

Without warning, Marty slapped the old man across the face, the sound echoing through the store.

"I want you to listen to me," Marty told him.

Marty backhanded him hard, drawing another cry from the old guy.

"You listening?"

The old man nodded. "Yes," he managed.

"You never saw me today," Marty said. "You never saw me at all. Get it?"

The old man bobbed his head, fear dulling his eyes.

"'Cause if the cops ever get us together again, and you show even a little that you might know me, I'll kill you. Nobody goes to jail very long for this kind of bullshit business, so I'll be back. You understand?"

The old man bobbed his head again.

"Good," Marty told him. "You just stay down there a while."

Marty gave the old man a final, vicious kick in the side. The old man moaned and fell back on the floor.

Marty hurried around the counter and made his way to the door where Stevie was waiting for him. They left the store and headed back to the car, moving at a good pace but not running.

"Did you have to hurt the old guy like that?" Stevie asked.

"Shut up."

In less than two minutes, they were back in the Civic. Marty pulled the amusement park gift cards and the cash register money from his pockets and handed them to Stevie.

"Count it," he ordered.

As Stevie began counting, Marty got the car started, pulled out of the parking spot, and headed down the street.

"How much?" Marty asked, his tone impatient.

"Just a second."

Stevie shuffled through the bills and then sighed.

"There's only sixty-eight bucks here."

"Are you kidding me?" Marty almost exploded.

"That's all," Stevie said.

"Shit," Marty said. "This penny ante crap is killing me. I'm never gonna get out of here at this rate."

"What're we gonna do?" Stevie asked, his voice timid.

"Let me think, will ya?"

They drove in silence for a few minutes. Marty had no idea where he was heading.

"There's sixty bucks worth of Oceanside Park gift cards," Stevie said, hoping the added value would make a difference.

"Can we spend that sixty, you idiot?"

"No."

Marty started thinking about those cards, and the more he thought, the more he liked the idea that was forming.

"A lot of money changes hands in that place. In any amusement park it does," he mused. "I think this looks like a nice day to spend at Oceanside."

"We're going to Oceanside?" Stevie asked with childlike enthusiasm.

"We disappear in the crowd and keep an eye out for any easy money at the same time," Marty continued. "With any luck, by tonight I might have enough for me to get the hell out of this city."

"I guess it was kind of like destiny that you scored the passes, then," Stevie said, pleased.

"Yeah, destiny, that's it."

CHAPTER FOUR
OCEANSIDE PARK

M arty took in the sights as he and Stevie walked under the intersecting, twenty-foot arches supporting a towering statue of King Neptune. The warm weather had brought a sizeable crowd out to Oceanside Park, and that was good for a lot of reasons.

A cacophony of music and the mechanical din from the different amusements cascaded over parents with their snot-nosed kids, teenagers that ran from ride to ride, servicemen and women strolling along in small groups, and the thirty-somethings hoping to revive some of their childhood memories.

Marty was quite proud of his idea. The park would be a good place to hang out for the rest of the day. It was an L-shaped twenty-five acres running along the shoreline and making a right angle onto the huge pier extending over the bay. Yeah, it was a good place to get lost in.

"Hand over your pass," Marty instructed Stevie.

Stevie reached into his shirt pocket and withdrew the park gift card. Marty pulled his card, and the two extras he had stolen, and threw all of them into a nearby trash bin.

"If anybody asks, we paid cash to get in, get it?" Marty said.

"Yeah, sure," Stevie nodded.

They took their time, strolling through the crowd, enjoying the cool breeze blowing in from the water.

"Rides are included in the entrance fee," Marty said. "But a bunch of the walk-through attractions charge admission. We'll check out those, and maybe some of the concessions."

"Okay," Stevie said.

"If we do things right, we might be able to hit two or three ticket booths, or a concession stand register drawer before we get out of here tonight," Marty said. "A little planning, some good timing. It'll all work out."

"I don't know," Stevie said, not even trying to disguise his nervousness. He pulled a plastic bottle out of his pants pocket, twisted off the cap, pulled out a couple of tablets, and popped them in his mouth.

"Don't start that shit on me," Marty said. "I told you. We just have to be careful. We'll be okay."

Stevie, unconvinced, stuffed the bottle back in his pants.

"I just need a little push," Stevie said.

They were walking around the back of the Ferris wheel when Marty glimpsed two blue uniforms through the crowd. He hooked Stevie's arm and moved around to the other side of the ride.

"What the hell, Marty?" Stevie asked.

"Over there, by the diving bell ride," Marty pointed. "My old pal Officer Larkin, and his partner."

"You're friends with that guy?" Stevie asked in surprise.

"No, stupid, but he knows me," Marty answered. "Come on."

Marty started moving, but not fast enough. He saw Larkin looking their direction, trying to get a better view through the crowd.

"This way," Marty instructed, heading towards the ocean side of the park.

They moved along, trying not to draw any attention by hurrying too fast. Up ahead was the Ocean Skyway ride, bubble-shaped gondolas suspended seventy-five feet above the ocean surface. It would carry them a good half mile out to sea and back, and give them a good vantage point at the same time.

Marty pulled Stevie into the line with him. He looked back and saw Larkin and his partner in the distance, scanning the crowd. The cops didn't see them in the line, but it wouldn't be long before they did. A group of tourists joined the line, blocking the line of sight between them and the cops. It would buy them a little time.

The line moved quickly and in a few minutes they were in one of the bubble cars being lifted into the air. The land beneath them morphed into the glistening surface of the sea. Marty looked back through the plexiglass. Larkin and the other cop were still strolling, looking through the crowd. They hadn't seen them board the ride.

Below them, off to one side, the big Oceanside Park pier extended over the bay for some three hundred yards. Marty gazed down upon the many pier concession stands where you could buy chocolate-dipped frozen bananas, hot pretzels, popcorn, hamburgers and hot dogs, and ice cream. There were also a couple of nice restaurants and a bunch of souvenir shops, all selling the same overpriced junk.

He had a clear view of the three rides on the pier as well. He remembered the Mystery Island Banana Train from his first trip to the park years earlier. It carried passengers through a tropical jungle and featured some kind of simulated earthquake. There was the Mahi Mahi, a high tower with two rotating arms, each holding a rocket-shaped car that carried several passengers, swinging them out over the water. At the very end of the pier was one of the park's two roller coasters, giving its riders a thrilling view over the expanse of ocean.

In five minutes, they reached the last tower and the bubble car headed back towards shore. In another five minutes, Marty was scanning the crowd as they began descending. There was no sign of the cops.

With their feet back on solid ground, Marty and Stevie headed inland again. Marty knew they'd have to be watchful, but he felt pretty confident that they had shaken the cops. Only ten minutes after exiting the Ocean Skyway, Marty spotted Larkin and his partner again through the crowd.

"This way, Stevie, come on," he said, changing his direction.

"I see 'em," Stevie said.

Marty set a course for the bumper cars, glancing nervously over his shoulder. He couldn't be sure, but it looked like Larkin was looking at him, or trying to, through the throng of people. And then he was sure. Larkin tapped his partner on the arm and then turned in their direction.

Marty moved a little faster, looking for routes that would put something between him and the cops. He and Stevie made their way to the opposite side of the bumper cars. Marty paused, peering across the canopied arena to the other side, trying to get eyes on the cops. There they were, looking this way and that, trying to figure out where he was. Suddenly, they started walking again, heading right for him.

"They're coming," Marty reported.

"We need another ride," Stevie said, looking around, desperate for a place to go. "There," he pointed.

Marty turned around to look.

About fifty feet away was a building with a facade made to look like ancient stones. At each end were castle-like towers, designed to look as if they might tumble down at any moment. The roof arched between the two towers, sheltering the two-seated cars running along the track below. A large demon's head with a gaping mouth, made to look like carved stone, decorated the center of the arch, just below its peak. Below the head, painted in large, bold faded red lettering, was the name: INFERNO GHOST TRAIN. And in smaller lettering below that, DARK RIDE.

"Come on," Stevie urged, taking a few steps towards the dark ride.

Marty didn't move, his eyes searching for some other place they could go. The screams from the teenage girls, as their cars pushed past the ride entrance, reached him over the noise of the crowd.

"Come on," Stevie pushed. "Those cops'll be here in a minute."

"You go. I'll meet you somewhere after," Marty told him.

Stevie looked at him, studying him. "Are you afraid?"

Marty felt himself flush as he stepped over to Stevie and grabbed him by his shirt.

"I'm not afraid of anything," he answered. "Sure as hell not a kiddie ride."

He let go of Stevie and turned to see if he could see Larkin and his partner. There they were, halfway around the bumper car perimeter.

"It's just that I don't like these dark rides," Marty continued. "Never have. Maybe it's something from when I was a kid."

"You better get over it, fast," Stevie said. "We're out of time."

The cops were almost at a point where they'd be in sight.

Stevie headed for the dark ride and got in line. There were only two couples ahead of him.

Marty saw nowhere else to go and felt a tremor of panic. Stevie moved up in the line. He'd get the next car. Marty hurried over and joined him.

"Good," Stevie said. "We'll lose 'em now."

Marty felt a strange feeling wash over him. He looked over at the ride operator and was startled to see the man staring at him.

More startling was that Marty was certain he knew the guy. It was the fortune teller freak from the police station the day before. But it couldn't be. This guy was at least twenty-five years older.

But the added years in the craggy face were the only difference. The penetrating eyes and hawkish features were the same. The tall, bony frame and messy strands of hair across the prominent forehead were identical. And then there was that long, dark coat.

"What're you lookin' at?" Marty challenged.

The ride operator widened his odd smile as the empty ride car rolled into place and stopped with a mechanical clacking sound and the hiss of hydraulics.

"I know you," Marty stated as he joined Stevie in the car.

The sound of maniacal laughter rumbled out of the dark tunnel in front of the car.

"Do you?" the ride operator answered, his voice low and even.

Before Marty could say another word, the ride operator pushed down the car's safety bar, anchoring them both in the seat. He extended a long, bony finger and punched a button on the console. The button light flashed from red to green and the car lurched forward into the darkness.

CHAPTER FIVE
FIRST RIDE

Marty heard the double doors hiss shut behind him and gripped the car's safety bar even tighter. The darkness swept in around him, cold and oppressive. The sound of screams from people in the cars ahead of him, combined with the din of horrific sounds coming from the ride's speaker system, made him want to scream. But he didn't, he couldn't. Even his throat was paralyzed with fear.

Pairs of glowing red eyes appeared bodiless in the darkness, while moans and growls screeched from the speakers. Ahead, a body of a man suddenly dropped into view, the noose around its neck forcing the neck to an impossible angle, the mouth of the victim forced open in a silent cry of agony.

"Marty. You okay?" he heard Stevie ask.

Why did Stevie have to notice him like this? Why did he have to ask questions?

"Marty?" Stevie called out again.

Forcing himself, Marty turned his head towards Stevie.

Stevie was staring at him with confused eyes.

Marty couldn't stand that look and turned away, facing forward again, closing his eyes tight against what might be next.

A sudden rush of cold air forced him to open his eyes. The car was speeding him towards a group of hideous, ghostly monsters that reached for him from both sides of the track.

Blood dripped from their mouths and their long, clawlike mechanical fingers opened and closed as they moved to grab him.

Stevie laughed aloud as the car moved past the horrible creatures. "So bad!" Stevie laughed again. "They look so damn fake."

Marty wondered if Stevie was even looking at the same thing he was. Why couldn't he see it? Why was he so blind?

"It's almost done, Marty," he heard Stevie say. "The ride's almost over."

Marty shuffled in great discomfort. Why was it getting so hot? Beads of sweat dripped down into his eyes. It stung and he wanted to wipe it away, but he'd have to let go of the safety bar, and that he couldn't bring himself to.

A deep red glow cut through the blackness. Hidden red spotlights focused on cellophane flames that flickered all around the car. The mechanically animated dummies of men and women could be seen among the flames, their faces grotesque from the tormenting fire. Anguished cries cascaded from the audio system.

Fear had consumed him from the moment the car had lurched into the dark tunnel, but now a fresh torrent of intensified dread took hold.

"It's not real, it's not real," he heard the words blurt from his mouth.

"It's almost over," he heard Stevie say again. "We're almost done, Marty."

Marty whimpered as a large spider, its body the size of volleyball, dropped into view on a very visible wire. It was a ridiculous thing, with red lit eyes that blinked on and off, and drooping, lifeless legs covered in some kind of bristly fabric. But the idea of any spider so large was revolting and horrifying to him. He recoiled from it as the car rolled past.

As the spider rose back into its hiding place, a growl, low and vicious, tore through the darkness above him. Marty found his head jerking upward as it grew louder. He couldn't stop himself from looking for the source of that terrible sound.

The Devil, huge, leaned down from the wall of plaster rocks ahead. Its heavy rubber skin was an ugly brownish gray, and dark wings on its shoulders flapped up and down. The grotesque, scaly face tilted left and right while the reptilian eyes glowed ember red.

The car sped for the black opening in the plaster rock below the Devil. Marty tried to sink down in his seat but the Devil reached down towards him.

"Nooo!" Marty cried out as the car plunged into the darkness.

There was a last, jarring turn, and then the double exit doors burst open before them. Marty struggled to force up the safety bar before the car had moved into the sunshine.

"It's okay, Marty. It's okay," Stevie said again.

The car slowed and there was the familiar clacking as the mechanism released the safety bar. Marty scrambled out of the car as quickly as he could, pausing only to get his bearings. At the front of the ride, the old ride operator still gazed at him, his face emotionless.

Marty hurried away past the guardrails until he was away from the front of the ride.

"Did you see it? Did you see it?" Marty asked as Stevie caught up with him.

Stevie stared at him, appearing very nervous. Marty could see the jerk didn't know what he was talking about.

"See what?" Stevie asked.

"That devil back in there, it reached for me," Marty wheezed, fighting to catch his breath.

"It's just all hokum, Marty," Stevie said. "It's just a crappy carnival ride."

"Did you see it? Marty almost screamed. "It reached for me."

"No, man, I'm sorry. I didn't see anything."

"It reached for me."

Stevie was silent for a while, wondering what he should say next.

Marty didn't want to, but he couldn't help himself, and glanced back towards the ride. The ride operator was still looking at him. Marty could see his head and those eyes through the crowd of people in the ride line. What was it with that asshole? It gave him the creeps.

"Let's get out of here," Marty said, breaking into a fast walk.

"What happened, man? What happened in there?" Stevie asked.

"I told you I didn't like those dark rides," Marty answered, his tone testy. "I've never liked them."

"Okay, okay, but it's all fake," Stevie said.

Marty whirled angrily towards Stevie and gave him a powerful shove. Stevie stumbled back, but Marty caught him by his flailing arm and jerked him back upright.

"I know it's all fake!" Marty shouted.

A couple of college kids and a group of Navy guys passing nearby stopped and stared.

Marty glanced at them for a brief, uncomfortable moment, and then started walking again.

"I know it's all fake," Marty repeated, his tone subdued.

"Okay, but—"

"Just shut it, man," Marty interrupted. "Let's find something to eat."

CHAPTER SIX
NAPKIN MONEY

Marty glanced around the sixties themed diner they'd decided on for lunch. The park had plenty of places to eat, but he remembered this one from a visit he'd made after hitting town five years ago. It pleased him to discover his memory was accurate. The burgers were juicy and the fries crisp. The vintage jukebox dropped the needle on "Stand by Me" as he raised his burger up to his mouth for another bite.

Across the table, Stevie was using a French fry to draw a smiley face in a big dollop of ketchup.

"Feeling better?" Stevie asked him after popping the fry in his mouth.

"I'm fine. Now just drop it. I don't want any more talk about it," Marty said, his voice fused with angry embarrassment.

"Okay, okay," Stevie said.

Stevie swallowed another French fry.

"You mind if I ask you a question?" Stevie asked.

"Depends."

"I keep wondering about your dad," Stevie said.

"That's more than I do," Marty sighed.

"I can't figure why you'd wanna walk away from being a big shot in that company. Maybe even owning it some day. You think you might've owned it someday?"

"All I wanted to do was get away from there," he said.

"Yeah, but it had to be crazy good pay, and you're only answering to your old man," Stevie reasoned.

"Too many hoops to jump through and too much work," he said.

"But what about college?" Stevie queried.

"What about it?"

"Didn't you want to stick around at least long enough to have your dad pay for college? I wanted to go to college, but my folks never had no money," Stevie said.

"Who says I didn't?" he challenged.

"You went to college?"

"A couple of years. That was enough for me," he answered.

Marty saw no reason to mention he'd been thrown out of college, and it'd been all over some girl. She'd been hot, and she'd been a big tease. When it came down to it, the little tease pretended she didn't want him. It got a little rough and afterwards the girl claimed he forced her. What bullshit, but they expelled him anyway.

"What was wrong with college?" Stevie asked.

"Too many people telling me what to do. What I can't do."

Marty took another bite of his burger and let his gaze drift to the crowd moving past the diner's picture window. His eyes weren't focused on anything particular on the other side of the window, not until he saw the dark blue uniforms.

"Damn it!" he cursed, tensing.

"What?" Stevie looked out the window.

"Give me your share of the money from this morning," Marty ordered, keeping his voice low. "Just keep like five bucks."

"What?"

"Larkin and that partner of his are heading this way," Marty said. "It could be a problem if they find the money on us."

Stevie dug into his pants pocket.

"Hurry it up!"

Stevie passed the few bills he had left across the table and then pulled the bottle of pills from his pocket, stuffing it down between the booth's Naugahyde seat cushion and the wall. Marty grabbed the napkin dispenser and pulled it into his lap.

He looked around. No one was paying much attention. Holding

out just enough to pay for the burgers, he combined Stevie's bills with his own. Prying open the napkin dispenser, he stuffed the bills behind the napkins at the very back of the holder and replaced the cover. He got the dispenser back on the table just as the bell above the door tinkled.

Larkin and his partner let the door close behind them and then looked around the room. Spotting him, Larkin got a big smile on his face. He nudged his partner and they headed over.

"Well, Marty Wedlow, as I live and breathe," Larkin said as he reached the table. "See, Oscar, I told you I thought I saw Marty heading this way."

"So you did," Romero responded.

"Mind if we join you a minute?" Larkin asked, sitting down in the booth across from him without waiting for an answer.

A waitress passing by with an order paused next to Romero.

"Bring you guys anything?" she asked.

"Nah, we're fine, thanks," Romero told her.

She hurried off to a table at the far end of the room.

"Who's this?" Larkin nudged Stevie with his elbow.

"Stevie," Stevie mumbled, his nerves obvious.

"Stevie what?" Romero asked, standing beside the table.

"Bander. Stevie Bander."

"You ever been arrested, Stevie?" Romero asked.

"Couple of times. Possession," Stevie answered, very unhappy.

"You a friend of Marty's?" Larkin asked.

"Yeah, I guess," Stevie answered.

"He's not sure," Romero smiled.

"We hang out sometimes," Marty said, doing his best to match Larkin's smile.

"So where were you guys hanging out this morning around ten?" Larkin asked.

"We were on our way here," Marty said. "Wanted to get an early start on all this fun."

"Is that right, Stevie?" Romero asked.

"Yeah."

"Make any stops?" Larkin continued.

"Like where?" Marty asked.

"You gonna make me ask you again?" Larkin said with less of a smile.

"No stops. Like I said, we wanted to get an early start on all the fun," Marty repeated. "What's this all about?"

"There was a nasty little robbery over on Ashford," Larkin explained. "You know Ashford?"

"Sure," Marty answered.

"Whoever did it is one big loser," Larkin said. "I mean, all they grabbed was some sixty bucks."

"No perp with any class would've even bothered," Romero observed. "Not worth the effort."

"You're looking at us for this?" Marty asked, measuring the surprise in his voice. "Why?"

"A few reasons," Larkin answered. "First, it's just the kind of shit you pull, and that store is less than two miles from here. And something else was stolen besides the cash."

"Any idea what that might be?" Romero asked.

"No," Marty answered, keeping his eyes on Larkin.

"Four gift card passes to Oceanside Park," Larkin told him.

"But there's just the two of us who came," Stevie blurted out.

"Shut up," Marty snapped.

"Technology today, it's really something," Larkin said.

"You finally figure out how to use your smart phone?" Marty jibed.

"See, we got the receipt for those passes from our robbery victim. What's the name again, Oscar?"

"Baumgarten," Romero answered.

"Save your breath," Marty said. "We paid cash to get in."

"Baumgarten, right," Larkin ignored him. "We got it from his wife, but it doesn't matter. What does matter is that the serial numbers for each pass were printed right on the receipt."

"But that's not the cool technology part," Romero chimed in.

"We stopped by the main gate on our way in here and had them type those serial numbers into their system," Larkin said. "And you know what? They told us two of those four stolen passes were used today. That's what I meant about the technology. Cool, huh?"

"That's some coincidence, you two being here the same morning," Romero said.

"I already told you, we paid cash," Marty insisted.

"So this loser, or maybe losers," Larkin continued with a glance towards Stevie. "They beat up the store owner. No reason for it. He gave them what they wanted, but they beat him anyway. An old man, they beat him up pretty bad."

"Gee, I hope he's gonna be all right," Marty said with just the right amount of sympathy.

"Me, too," Larkin said, sliding back out of the booth, his tone more sober.

"Leaving so soon?" Marty asked.

"Get up, both of you," Larkin ordered.

Stevie shot him a questioning look across the table. Marty shrugged and nodded. As they got to their feet, he noticed Romero step back a couple of paces, resting his hand on the grip of his Glock.

"Stand still," Larkin said to Stevie, as he began patting him down.

Larkin finished and did the same to Marty. Marty could feel the eyes of the people in the diner staring at him. He didn't like it and he felt the heat of anger flaming up inside him.

"Find anything good?" Marty asked, hearing the tenseness in his voice.

"Empty your pockets," Larkin ordered. "Put the contents on the table."

Marty fished in his pockets and dropped his car keys and some loose change on the table. Stevie contributed more change and a half-empty pack of gum.

"Wallets, take them out," Larkin said.

Marty took his time digging his wallet from his back pocket and offered it to Larkin.

"No, you keep it," Larkin instructed. Take out the bills and count them onto the table where I can see.

Marty shrugged and did as he was told. "Seventeen bucks," he reported.

Larkin turned to Stevie.

"I just got a five," Stevie told him, displaying the bill.

Larkin and Romero exchanged glances, and Marty felt good seeing the frustration on their faces.

"Okay, you can gather up your stuff," Larkin said.

Marty and Stevie began picking up their belongings.

"No stolen money. No park guest passes. No evidence at all," Marty said, sympathy in his tone. "Probable cause is a bitch, huh?"

Larkin said nothing, but Marty recognized the anger in his hard stare.

"When you're right, you're right," Larkin began. "I don't have enough probable cause to arrest you on suspicion of robbery. But I sure as hell have enough to get a warrant to search that room of yours."

"If you want to waste your time, who am I to stop you?" Marty shrugged.

"Still live in that flop house on Windward?" Larkin asked as he and his partner turned and headed out of the diner.

Marty felt the scowl mask his face as he dropped the money he had shown the cops on the table to cover the check. Watching through the diner's large window, he waited until they disappeared into the crowd.

"We gotta get back to my place," Marty told Stevie as he hurried toward the exit.

Stevie caught up and followed him through the door.

"But why?" Stevie asked. "I like it here."

"I've still got a couple of things at my place from that B and E job I told you about. If Larkin gets lucky and gets that warrant, the stuff in my room can tie me to the job."

"Well, are we coming back?" Stevie asked.

"I don't know," Marty answered. "The cops are screwing this all up."

Stevie looked devastated.

"Geez, don't have a fit. We'll get our hands stamped on the way out, just in case we come back."

CHAPTER SEVEN
MARTY'S OLD FRIENDS

M arty approached his boarding house from the rear and parked the Civic around the corner. His memory clicked in the moment he slammed the car door.

"Son of a bitch," he cursed.

"What?" Stevie asked.

"We left our money back there. Our money from the store is back in that diner. Son of a bitch!"

"And my dexies," Stevie exclaimed, his memory catching up and his panic obvious. "I pushed 'em down in the corner of the booth."

"Damn cops," Marty growled. "We gotta go back there. As soon as we finish up here, we'll go back."

"Yeah, we need to go back," Stevie agreed.

Marty led the way to the back of the building. They passed the building's dumpsters, climbed the few steps leading into the main hallway, and then climbed the back stairway up to the third floor.

Once inside his room, Marty went to the electric wall heater. He removed the four screws fastening the front cover screen to the heater. As he pulled the screen away from the wall, two expensive men's wristwatches fell onto the dirty carpet.

"Put these in your pocket." Marty handed the watches to Stevie.

"Wow, thanks."

"Just make sure nothing happens to them. I'll get 'em from you later," Marty told him as he refastened the screen cover to the heater.

Marty locked the door behind him and they left the building by the same route by which they'd entered.

They were heading back to the car when two men suddenly appeared around the corner directly ahead of them. Marty recognized them in an instant.

"Shit," he exclaimed under his breath, looking for a place where he could duck out of sight.

"What's wrong?" Stevie asked.

The leader of the two, Andy, was now looking his way. In another moment his confederate, Gene, spotted him as well. Both of them stared with expressions of surprise. And then the surprise turned to recognition. They hurried towards him.

The two thugs were between him and the car, so Marty bolted towards the opposite side of the street. Stevie cried out his name and then broke into a run behind him, barely avoiding an oncoming pickup truck that blared its horn at him.

Marty cut between two parked cars and headed for the nearest side street. He turned onto the street, scanning the path ahead for anyplace he might disappear. Stevie caught up to him.

"Marty," he wheezed. "What's going on?"

Marty glanced behind him. His pursuers entered the street at a full run.

"Go!" Marty ordered.

Together, they sprinted up the street. Marty led the way, dodging in and out of parked cars and around pedestrians. He wasn't used to this kind of thing and his lungs were already beginning to burn. And Stevie, he was just able to keep up.

Another glance behind him confirmed that Andy and Gene were closing the distance. Up ahead, Marty spotted an alley opening between two old brick buildings. He put on some extra speed and turned into the narrow passage with Stevie on his heels.

The alley cut through to the adjoining street and was empty of any other people or traffic.

Marty knew if he could make it to that next street he might have a chance of shaking the two men. He and Stevie ran hard. They passed a city roadwork project that jutted into the alley several feet, its striped barricades blocking off a large, jagged hole in the pavement.

They were almost to the end of the alley when Gene appeared in the street ahead, blocking their way. Marty stopped and turned. Running into the alley entrance behind them was Andy.

Marty and Stevie instinctively retreated from Gene, being the closest to them. They got only as far as the construction site before Andy reached them. Marty backed away from him, but a large pile of sand and a small cement mixer near the barricades stopped him in his tracks. Marty cursed to himself; a stupid pile of sand left them no place to go.

"We want our money, Marty," Andy spat.

"What're you talking about?" Marty asked.

"You thieving son of a bitch," Gene said.

"You got your money," Marty exclaimed.

Andy hurried at him, throwing a punch, but Marty got his arm up in time. The blow deflected off his forearm, but the force of it knocked him off balance and he hit the ground hard.

Stevie cowered back a few steps.

"What the hell, man?" Marty cried, climbing to his feet.

"Give us the money. And now we want all of it," Andy almost shouted.

"What money? I don't know what you're talking about," Marty insisted.

"You found more money in that house," Gene said. "A lot more than you split with us."

"That's crazy," Marty answered.

A knife appeared in Andy's hand. In another instant, he had hold of Marty's throat and the tip of the blade was under his chin.

Stevie turned to run, but Gene grabbed him before he could get far and held him in place.

"Enough of this shit," Andy growled. "You gave me and Gene seven hundred bucks from that job. You pulled it right out of that leather bag of yours and said that's all there was."

"Yeah. We each got seven hundred," Marty said.

Andy shoved him away hard and pointed the tip of the knife blade at him.

"You got almost three grand," Andy yelled.

"Marty," Stevie whimpered. "I didn't have nothing to do with any of this."

"Shut your mouth," Gene said, shoving him away hard.

Stevie stumbled into the sand pile and lost his balance. The clang of metal reverberated through the alley when Stevie's head connected with the side of the cement mixer. He crumpled into the sand and lay still.

"Damn, Gene," Marty breathed, looking down at Stevie.

"Don't worry about him," Andy snapped. "Maybe you shouldn't run your mouth so much if you're gonna try ripping me off."

"What're you talking—"

"You remember the night you stopped by the Pale Pelican?" Andy interrupted him.

Marty feigned not recognizing the name.

"That bar over on Everest Street."

"I don't know. Maybe," Marty answered, a bad feeling beginning to ooze into his system.

"Maybe, my ass," Andy continued. "You did a little celebrating and you got plastered. And then you did some bragging to the guy sitting next to you at the bar. Remember now?"

Marty had heard that word of what he'd done had gotten back to Andy. Now it was confirmed.

"Yeah, I see you remember. It's a really small world, Marty. That guy you mouthed off to is a friend of mine," Andy said.

"Geez, man. If I was loaded, I could've been talking a load of crap," Marty argued.

"But you weren't," Andy hissed. He jumped forward, grabbed Marty around the throat, backing him to the opposite side of the alley until he slammed into the brick wall.

A sharp pain shot through the back of his head and Marty gasped to get air back into his lungs.

Gene joined them, taking a position beside Andy.

"Now, give me the money," Andy ordered. "All of it."

"Okay, okay," Marty wheezed. "I don't have it anymore."

"Sure you do," Gene said, venom in his tone.

"Honest, I don't. I went through it fast," Marty said.

"You went through it," Andy repeated.

"I swear, I swear I don't have it," Marty said. "My car got transmission problems. I had to use the cash to get it fixed. My wheels, man. Gotta have them."

"That didn't cost any three thousand," Andy said.

"The rest, the rest I partied some with it, and I lost most of it at the track," Marty said.

Andy's face flushed red with anger.

"You don't have any of it?" Gene cried.

Marty shook his head.

"You'll pay, Marty," Andy said.

Marty believed it and felt the cold needles of fear pricking at him. He didn't like the look in Andy's eyes.

"I'll pay it back, all of it," Marty promised, hearing the desperation in his voice.

"How you gonna do that?" Andy asked.

"I'll pull some jobs. It's easy," Marty told him. "You'll get it all, every cent."

Andy glared at him, but Marty could tell he was thinking about the offer. And then Andy's eyes narrowed and hardened.

"You're full of shit, Marty," Andy said. "You'll pull some jobs, and then you'll use it to get your thieving ass out of town. No, you're gonna have to pay."

Andy raised the knife again.

"No, Andy, I swear. I swear I'll pay you back every cent," Marty assured.

"You gonna kill him?" Gene asked, concerned.

Andy hesitated before answering. "Nah, but I'm gonna cut him enough so nobody'll want to look at him."

"No, Andy. Please..." Marty pleaded. The escalating fear had him close to tears.

"I gotta make an example of you, Marty. If I don't, I'll have everybody in town walking all over me."

A movement behind Andy and Gene drew Marty's gaze away from the knife, and they turned to see what he was looking at. Marty closed his eyes tight as Stevie hurled two fists of sand at them.

Andy and Gene screamed. Andy released his grip on Marty and

dropped the knife, raising his arm to cover his eyes. Gene was spinning in circles as he wiped his eyes with the back of his hands.

Marty felt his fear replaced by blind anger. He wound up and put everything he had behind a punch to Andy's jaw. Andy stumbled backward with a growl of pain but stayed on his feet. A vicious kick to his groin brought him down to his knees.

"Marty!" Stevie cried.

Marty spun around to see Gene blindly grappling with Stevie. Stevie was kicking and punching, but the bigger man wouldn't let go.

Marty hit Gene hard on the side of the head and followed through by shoving him hard across the alley. Gene's legs went out from under him. With a cry of pain, he careened into one of the construction barricades, knocking it into the shallow hole and tumbling in after it.

A groan behind him made Marty turn. Andy, on his knees, was crawling towards the knife. Marty covered the distance quickly, delivered a kick to Andy's side, and laid him out flat. Marty snatched up the knife and then searched Andy until he found the leather sheath tucked into the waistband of his jeans.

"Come on," Marty shouted to Stevie, sliding the sheathed knife into his own waistband and covering it with his shirt.

They both ran toward the end of the alley. They were halfway there when Marty glanced back to see Andy staggering to his feet and Gene pulling himself from the hole. Both of them began scuttling up the alley in pursuit.

Marty and Stevie reached the end of the alley and rounded the corner. The Civic was parked up the block and they raced for it.

As they approached the car, Marty pulled out his keys. He struggled to get the key into the lock.

"Marty!" Stevie cried.

Closing in on them, Andy and Gene came running up the sidewalk.

Marty got the key in the lock and pulled open the door. He threw himself behind the wheel and got the key into the ignition, opening the passenger door for Stevie at the same time.

He glanced in the rear view mirror. Andy and Gene were almost on them.

Marty turned the key. He felt genuine relief when the engine turned over with no problem.

Andy and Gene reached the car as Marty got the Civic into gear and pushed down on the accelerator. The car shuddered when the two men, mad with fury, slammed their fists onto the trunk as the car pulled away.

Marty swerved into traffic, narrowly missing another car, and then gave the Civic more gas. He felt his heartbeat slow as he watched the two men grow smaller and smaller in the rear view mirror.

CHAPTER EIGHT
BACK AT THE DINER

Marty parked the Civic in the Oceanside Park lot and hurried his way back towards the main gate with Stevie on his heels.

"Those guys back there. They're why you want to leave town, right? Stevie asked.

Marty knew the encounter in the alley shook Stevie up. He'd remained quiet during the ride to the park, and that was unlike him. Marty had been wondering when Stevie might calm down enough to say something about what happened.

"They're as good a reason as any," Marty answered, not liking the question.

Reaching the return entrance gate, the attendant scanned their hand stamps and waved them into the park.

"I'm glad we came back," Stevie said.

"We didn't have much choice. We have to get what's ours," Marty replied. "Besides, with everything that's gone down, nobody will think to look for me in here."

"You mean those guys," Stevie said.

"Just forget them. We're here and I'm not leaving this place until tonight. And I'm leaving with some real money."

"Okay, Marty."

There were more people in the park now and the sun was a little hotter. They were halfway to the diner when Marty moved to the side of the thoroughfare and rested his shoulder against the side of a spin-paint booth.

"Look there," he pointed.

"What?" Stevie asked, unsure what he was looking for.

"Right there, see the sign? *Journey to the Deep*," Marty read. "It's one of those walk-through attractions."

"Okay."

The exhibit building was ocean green with a mural of strange and monstrous sea creatures covering the entire facade. It was a skillfully crafted mural with the fantastic creatures painted to look as they might really exist. But the paint was now faded and peeling.

The neighboring attraction was a Tilt-a-Whirl ride, the happy screams and shouts from its riders rising above the music coming through the park sound system.

"It's got a ticket booth, so there's a separate admission charge," Marty explained. "And it's doing some business. Look at the line."

"Yeah, busy," Stevie said.

"See there, the right side of the booth connects to the exhibit building. There's no door on the left side, so you get into it either from inside the building or at the back," Marty said. "See, the back of the booth is set out from the building wall, maybe six feet."

"What's that mean?" Stevie asked.

"Wait here."

Marty strolled towards the Tilt-a-Whirl ride, feigning interest in the contraption. He kept walking until he was a few feet past the Journey to the Deep ticket booth and then turned around. He was right. There was a narrow passage between the building wall and the back of the booth, and a plain, wood door was set in the back wall of the booth. The Tilt-a-Whirl provided good cover from the opposite side, and once he was in the passage behind the ticket booth, nobody could see him from the front. It was perfect.

Marty made his way back to Stevie who waited for him with the usual confused expression on his face.

"This'll do fine," Marty reported.

"We're gonna hit it?" Stevie asked.

"Maybe around dinner time," Marty told him. "People'll be

getting hungry and taking a food break. We'll watch for the line to thin out."

"And it'll be dark," Stevie added.

"Not quite, but who cares? They won't be expecting it then."

"You think so?" Stevie asked with an obvious lack of confidence.

"I think so."

"How we gonna get out of here with the money?" Stevie probed further, lowering his voice.

Marty gave that one some thought. "We don't. We hide it and then just hang out here."

"Hide it?"

"We hang here out in the open, just having a nice day at Ocean-side Park," Marty elaborated. "We're good as long as we don't have the cash on us. Once it all calms down, we get the money and get out of here."

"You sure it'll work?" Stevie asked, his nerves showing again.

"Don't worry about it," Marty replied. "The diner's just over there. Let's go get our money."

They set out again, weaving through the throng. The closer Marty got to the diner, the faster he walked, and that pissed him off. He couldn't believe he was so hard up for money that he was rushing to get his hands on not much more than fifty bucks.

They reached the diner, and Marty hurried inside with Stevie on his heels. He made his way along the line of booths, his eyes fixed on the table where they'd had lunch. There it was, toward the end of the room. He slowed his pace so abruptly that Stevie bumped into him. There was someone in their booth, a man sitting with his back to them, his long, gray hair hanging across his coat collar.

"Hey, Marty, there's a guy—" Stevie began.

"Shut up," Marty interrupted. "I see him."

Marty knew exactly who it was as he approached the booth, with Stevie lagging a safe distance behind. He closed the distance to the table and stopped beside it.

The operator from the dark ride glanced up at them. On the table in front of him was a plate of chicken fried steak and a cup of coffee. Sitting beside the table's napkin dispenser was Stevie's little bottle of pills and a wad of folded cash.

CHAPTER NINE
MR. SABNOCK

The ride operator cut a slice of chicken fried steak, impaled it on the fork and popped it in his mouth.

"They do a good job with the chicken fried steak here," he said with his mouth full.

Marty hardly heard him; he was trying to decide what to do about the money. He knew it was possible the cash on the table belonged to this old man, but it looked like the money he'd folded into the napkin dispenser. Did that even make sense? One pile of money looking just like another.

"Are you looking for something?" the ride operator asked, his tone unconcerned.

Marty reached in front of the old guy and grabbed hold of the napkin dispenser. While the old guy took another bite of his lunch, Marty pulled the napkins out of the dispenser. All the damn thing had in it was napkins. He dropped the dispenser back on the table.

"You've made quite a mess," the ride operator observed.

"It looks like you found our money," Marty said.

The ride operator glanced at the cash.

"Why do you think it's yours?" he asked.

"I left it here," Marty answered, his voice tense.

"That seems odd," the ride operator said between bites. "Most people take their money with them when they leave a restaurant."

Every time this jerk opened his mouth, he sounded like he knew more than he was saying. Marty didn't know what he was trying to prove, but it was pissing him off.

Marty slipped into the seat across from the ride operator.

"What's your name, mister?" he asked.

"You can call me Sabnock," the old guy replied with a wolfish smile.

"Sabnock? What the hell kind of name is that?" Marty asked.

"An old one," Sabnock said, sliding another forkful of food into his mouth.

"So, where did you find that money, Mr. Sabnock?" Marty probed.

"Who said that I found it?"

"I asked you a question," Marty said, hearing the anger in his voice.

"I heard you," Sabnock replied.

"That money's mine," Marty said, reaching across the table for the cash.

Sabnock took hold of Marty's wrist so fast, Marty didn't even see him move. His bony fingers dug into Marty's flesh with an unnatural strength and there was a feeling, a strange, sickening feeling, as if his strength were being sucked out of him. Sabnock leaned forward, just a few inches, his dark, penetrating eyes daring Marty to meet his gaze.

"Finders keepers, losers weepers, Mr. Wedlow," Sabnock whispered without humor.

Marty glanced up at Stevie who was standing paralyzed, staring down at both of them with eyes as wide as saucers. He forced his eyes back to Sabnock.

"What's with you? How do you know my name?" Marty asked, trying to pull away from the old guy.

Sabnock let go of his wrist, picked up the pill bottle and offered it to Stevie.

"I think you'll be needing these," Sabnock smiled.

Stevie took the bottle with the tentativeness of a man afraid of being burned by a hot frying pan handle.

Sabnock then moved his hand over to the money, resting it on the folded bills. Without looking at the cash, he slid it from the table and into his coat pocket with a single, fluid motion.

"I'll be keeping the money," Sabnock said. "Let's call it a credit toward your next ride on the Inferno Ghost Train."

Marty didn't understand why, but he no longer felt like fighting about the money. It angered him to realize that he was afraid to fight with this weird old fart.

"I don't need any credit," was all he could think to say. "I'll never ride that thing again."

The chuckle that crackled from Sabnock's throat was so unnatural that it sent a chill up Marty's spine.

"Choices, choices, choices," Sabnock murmured, very congenial. "Everyone makes choices that set them on a path to their destinies."

"What're you talking about? Marty asked.

"Everyone loves a good, dark ride, Mr. Wedlow. You'll ride again."

Marty slid out of the booth and hovered over the old man, unable to discern his anger from his fear.

"I'm not gonna forget this," he hissed. "I'm not gonna forget you, Mr. Sabnock."

Sabnock again leveled his dark eyes on him, taking in every inch of his body as if trying to guess his weight and height.

"Nor should you, Mr. Wedlow, nor should you," Sabnock replied.

CHAPTER TEN
THE TICKET BOOTH ROBBERY

Marty leaned on the pier railing, watching the sun sink lower in the summer sky. The horizon was an orange-red and the sunlight glittered off the ocean's undulating surface. In the distance, people enjoyed the beach - couples holding hands, teens throwing Frisbees, and families with their children. Maybe a dozen surfers were sitting on their boards some hundred yards off the shore, waiting for a wave.

His mind wasn't on all the fun in the sun. What interested him was the Journey to the Deep exhibit, which he could see from his vantage point on the railing. Fewer and fewer people had been getting in the line. It wouldn't be long now and that ticket taker would be all by himself.

He glanced at the bronze plaque mounted on the railing next to him. The plaque inscription explained that the original pier was constructed in 1908 and was located just north of the current location. A mysterious fire destroyed it in 1969 and some of the original pilings were still visible. The oceanfront acreage remained vacant for over ten years until the Tartan Amusements Corporation acquired the property to develop Oceanside Park.

Stevie, slipping his bottle of pills out of his pocket, drew his attention.

"Put those away," Marty ordered.

"Just one, Marty, please. I need a little something. Just one."

"Just one, then put 'em away."

Stevie rolled a capsule out of the bottle and popped it in his mouth. He fumbled the top back on the bottle and put it back in his pocket.

"My dad used to take us to the beach," Stevie said, pointing at one family in the distance.

"Yeah? My dad used to take my brother and me to the plant and tell us how he expected us to toe the line," Marty said.

"You have a brother?" Stevie sounded surprised.

"I just said so."

"Older or younger?"

"Older by three years."

"You ever see him anymore?" Stevie asked.

"He's got no interest in seeing me. Last time I heard he was still living in Delaware," Marty answered. "Still working for the old man in the business."

"I'd like to see my folks, but the times I do they always give me grief about rehab, getting a decent job, you know," Stevie sighed.

The line was down to a half-dozen people now. Lights on the amusements and along the thoroughfares began coming on.

Marty shifted his position and gazed over the railing at the beach below. Gentle waves rolled in and flowed around the grouping of old, charred pilings that once belonged to the original pier. Several of them looked to be quite sharp, their jagged, blackened points jutting out of the sand a few feet like a field of decrepit vampire stakes. He realized that the old pier must have been directly next to this new one. The beach would've looked a hell of a lot better if the pilings had been completely removed, he thought, but that would've cost a greedy corporation more money.

Marty pushed his attention back to the ticket booth. There were only three people in line. Now was as good a time as any.

"Let's go," Marty said.

"Now?" Stevie asked with both excitement and fear in his voice.

"Yeah."

They walked along the pier towards the shore. They hadn't gotten far when Marty stopped, his attention drawn to an open air souvenir stall. Several potential customers milled through its displays, and off to the side of the stall was a kiosk on which hung a variety of cheap vinyl shopping bags, all with the Oceanside Park name and logo on them.

"We're gonna need one of those bags," Marty pointed.

"Okay," Stevie agreed, not realizing why.

"Go get one of them."

"I've only got a few bucks left," Stevie whined. "I don't want to blow it on a plastic bag."

"You're not gonna need money," Marty assured him.

Stevie looked confused at the revelation, but soon figured it out.

"Oh, sure."

"Don't get caught. I'll be up ahead there," Marty told him.

Marty moved ahead as Stevie walked over to the souvenir stall and feigned browsing the displayed goods. It wasn't long before the throng of people blocked Stevie from his view. The bag was a little thing, but he didn't want to risk getting nailed for it. If Stevie blew it, then only he would get tossed out of the park. Marty would still have the chance to go after the money he needed.

But Stevie rejoined him in just a few minutes, an aqua green bag decorated with blue dolphins folded under his arm.

"Easy," he reported, pleased with himself.

Marty just nodded and continued on through the crowd. It didn't take long to return to the spin-paint booth across from the Journey to the Deep exhibit. He stood there for several minutes with Stevie at his side, fidgeting as usual, keeping an eye on the ticket booth. A few more people had lined up at the booth since they left the pier, but it was still a small number. He took a last look at the surrounding attractions and scanned the crowd for the cops or park security.

When the line dropped to three customers, he nudged Stevie.

"Get in the line," Marty told him. "Once you're up to the window, stand in front of it."

"But the guy inside'll get a square look at me," Stevie argued.

"Just look down a lot. And what if he does get a look at you? You're just a guy who wanted to buy a ticket. I'll be inside doing the work."

"I guess so," Stevie said, unconvinced.

The line was down to two people, and Marty didn't see anybody else heading for the ticket booth.

"Give me the bag," Marty said.

Stevie handed it over.

"Come on, but wait 'til I get behind the booth," Marty continued, moving forward.

Stevie dropped behind him and Marty made his way towards the ticket booth. He glimpsed the ticket taker through the ticket window, a young college-aged kid. Passing the front of the structure, he took a final look around. Nobody was paying any attention to him. He slipped behind the building and then edged to the side so he could look around to the front. Stevie's timing was good; he approached the front of the booth at that moment.

Marty turned to the door and wrapped his fingers around the handle. He tried to open the door, but it was locked shut. Marty cursed to himself, but wasn't going to turn away from this now. He thought for a moment and then knocked on the door.

"Yes, who is it?" a youthful voice came through the door.

"It's Benson, park security," Marty called out. "They sent me over with some extra ticket rolls."

Marty held his breath, waiting to discover if his bluff was realistic or an obvious lie.

"Hang on," the voice said.

He heard the bolt drawn and stepped to the side of the doorway. The door swung open and the clerk, not seeing anyone, leaned forward to get a better view.

Marty hit him in the jaw as hard as he could. The guy's hands shot up to his face as he staggered in the doorway. Marty shoved him back into the booth, followed him in, then whirled the clerk around and smashed his head into the nearest wall. The clerk hit the floor just as Marty pulled the door shut behind him.

"Son of a bitch, Marty cursed, glancing at his red, throbbing knuckles.

"Shit, Marty," Stevie whispered through the window.

Marty ignored him, turning his attention to the cash box sitting on the counter below the window, its lid open. He stepped over the unconscious kid and began transferring the money from the cash tray to the dolphin bag. He got a rough count as he cleaned out each of the tray partitions. It was smart to wait until the end of the day. The attraction had done good business. There was almost a thousand bucks here, maybe even a little more than a thousand. He dropped the last of the bills into the bag.

"We're out of here," he told Stevie. "Walk to the back."

Marty heard the ticket taker groan as he slipped out of the booth and closed the door. He was already strolling around the back of the Tilt-a-Whirl as Stevie joined him.

"You really put the hurt on that guy," Stevie said, not sounding happy.

"He'll live. Now just shut up about it."

Putting some distance between themselves and the ticket booth, Marty headed for the Ferris wheel. They got in line and in a few minutes were soaring upward. The topmost point of the wheel gave them a good view of the park and they could see the security guys already gathering around the ticket booth.

"That didn't take long," Stevie observed.

"The cops'll be there in another couple of minutes," Marty said as they began rotating towards the ground.

"We're gonna get out of here, right?" Stevie asked.

"They're gonna watch the exits now," Marty responded. "The cops and security'll search everybody who wants to leave. Nah, we're not going anywhere, at least for a while."

"Then what're we gonna do?"

"We're gonna find a place to hide this bag... and then we're gonna have some big fun at Oceanside Park."

CHAPTER ELEVEN
LARKIN'S BREAK

L arkin yawned as Romero turned their cruiser into the garage and headed for their parking space. The shift hadn't been too bad and he felt he had enough energy left for a good workout. He'd probably even get a second wind.

"Any thoughts on that last radio call?" Romero asked as he guided the cruiser into the parking space.

"What call was that?" Larkin asked, knowing full well what his partner was talking about.

They climbed out of the cruiser and walked around to the trunk. Romero popped it, and they pulled out their gear.

"The robbery out at Oceanside," Romero said, realizing Larkin was messing with him.

"I think Wedlow could be involved, if that's what you mean," Larkin replied.

Romero closed the trunk and locked the cruiser. They started walking towards the building entrance.

"If he was, he's gotta be the biggest idiot there is," Romero said. "Who goes and pulls jobs so close together when he knows the cops are looking at him so hard?"

"Something else is going on with him, desperate for money or something," Larkin said.

They pushed open the double doors leading from the garage into the building.

"What's cookin' Bill," Larkin greeted the uniformed officer behind the garage entrance security desk.

"Hi, Jack," Bill responded. "Don't get too relaxed."

"Yeah?"

"The Captain called down a couple of minutes ago," Bill explained. "He said to come see him soon as you got in."

"Uh oh," Romero chuckled.

"Both of you," Bill added. "Leave your gear with me. You can check it in when you're done."

"Come on, laughing boy," Larkin told Romero.

"Hey Jack," Bill called out after him. "My missus wants to know when you're going to marry that girl of yours. I think she wants a firm date."

"Yeah?" Larkin responded without turning around. "Well, tell her things have been a little hectic. I've had a lot of laundry to do, and then we've got the World Series coming up. Oh, and I've gotta make sure I can get her in on my gym membership."

The laughter behind him interrupted his flow.

They made their way down the hall to the elevator and took it up to the second floor. The Captain was standing in his office doorway giving instructions to his assistant when they reached his office.

"Larkin, Romero," the Captain greeted them.

"Heard you wanted to see us," Larkin said.

"Yeah, step in a minute," the Captain said, going back into his office.

They followed him in.

"You handled a robbery call this morning, a grocery store over on Ashford?"

"That's right," Larkin answered. "The owner got beat up pretty bad."

The Captain glanced down at a file on his desk. "Yeah, a Mr. Nathan Baumgarten. You like anybody for this?"

"A guy named Martin Wedlow," Larkin responded.

"Have you talked to him?"

"We talked to him," Larkin said. "I know he's good for it, but we don't have enough to do anything about it. I even threatened him with getting a warrant to shake his room, just to see if I'd get a reaction, but I didn't even have enough to do that."

"And did you get a reaction?"

"He tensed up quite a bit," Romero said.

"Well, this may be your lucky day," the Captain said. "When the detective interviewed Baumgarten this morning, he was scared, very scared. He told us he couldn't identify the perp, but it looks now like he's had a change of heart."

"Yeah?" Larkin said.

"The hospital called not ten minutes ago," the Captain explained. "The victim wants to talk to us again. You guys put together a six pack with your suspect's photo in it and go see our victim."

"You got it," Larkin answered. "But we just got off our shift. It'll mean overtime."

"Like I said," the Captain responded. "This is your lucky day."

CHAPTER TWELVE
THE GIRLS

"You're sure you didn't kill that guy," Stevie whispered, leaning across the table. "Right, Marty?"

"I just cracked his head a little," Marty replied.

This was the second time Stevie had asked the same question in the last ten minutes and normally it would've pissed him off. But tonight he felt good; he felt great. The ticket booth had netted him at least a thousand bucks. Good money, damn good money. The whole thing had gone off without any screw ups, too. It was good money too. Enough so he could get out of the city. It wasn't enough to keep him going for long, but it was enough for a start for his trip north. He'd leave tomorrow. He could always pick up more money on the way.

"I love fried clams," Stevie said, popping a forkful into his mouth, his expression of apprehension morphing into one of satisfaction.

"Yeah? This burger's good, too," Marty responded.

Their first order of business after leaving the Ferris wheel ride was to find a place to hide the money until the heat died down. Several police units had arrived, but their focus was on the ticket booth and getting reports from the park security people. Only a couple of officers were scanning the crowd, and it was easy for Marty to find ways around them while he looked for a place to stash the money.

It didn't take him long to spot a little kids' ride that was decorated with oversized flower pots holding oversized, colorful plastic flowers that lined the front of the ride. They worked their way around to the back of the building housing the ride where they found a few more of the big pots stored against a wall, all of them worn or damaged.

After pulling just enough cash out of the dolphin bag to get them through the rest of the evening, Marty stuffed the bag with the rest of the money through a large crack in one of the pots. He turned the cracked side of the pot to the wall and they got out of there.

Now they were kicking back at an open air restaurant, each of them with a beer, and the burger and clams. It had cooled down and there was a gentle breeze blowing in off the ocean.

"Why didn't you order the clams?" Stevie asked him. "They're great here."

"I'm not big on seafood," he answered. "Any of it."

Stevie considered this for a moment and then leaned across the table.

"Marty... how much do you think we got tonight?" Stevie asked in a whisper.

"I tried a rough count while I gathered it up," he replied, keeping his voice low. "I'd say we got about five hundred."

Stevie's eyes widened with excitement. "Five hundred? That's great!"

"Yeah, and that makes your take two hundred," Marty elaborated.

Stevie wrinkled his forehead up while he tried to figure out the math and ended up not looking happy.

"Two?" he asked.

"Hey, which one of us did the tough part?" Marty asked him.

Marty watched while Stevie thought about it. The guy had never gotten a good look at the money, so he didn't have a clue how much might be there. What he didn't know wouldn't hurt him.

"Nah, nah, you're right," Stevie said, sounding disappointed despite his agreeing.

Some movement from the front of the restaurant caught Marty's eye. The hostess was leading a couple of girls to a table about a dozen feet away.

"Holy shit," Marty exclaimed.

Stevie began rotating in his chair.

"No, don't look," Marty ordered.

"What?" Stevie froze, confused.

"A couple of girls just came in. One of them's dark and curvy. She's a pretty hot Latina. But shit, the other one," Marty breathed. "Blonde, tall and slender, tan all over. She's wearing these tight denim shorts. God have mercy."

Stevie was struggling to keep his eyes in front of him.

"Okay, check it out, but take your time, casual," Marty nodded toward the girls' table as they slid into their chairs.

"You don't know them?" Stevie asked, taking in the view.

"I'd like to know them," Marty answered, his eyes still on the blonde.

A purple streak ran down the side of her short, shaggy haircut. She looked to be in her early twenties, but that didn't matter.

"I know what you mean," Stevie said, turning his attention back to the clams.

Marty forced his eyes away from the blonde and took another bite of his burger. There was something about this girl, she was so his type.

Stevie leaned forward again. "Are we going after anymore money tonight?" he whispered.

"More is always better," Marty replied, feeling his eyes drifting back to the girl. "We're gonna be here a while. If I see something that might work for us, we'll go for it."

The girls shared a joke and their youthful, uninhibited laughter drifted over to him. Both of them had looks, but the blonde's smile had some real power.

"It's been a good day," he heard Stevie say across the table. "I mean, I didn't like those guys in the alley, but things've gone good, pretty much. If you see a chance for more cash, I think that'd go good, too."

Marty had to agree. The incident in the alley could've ended a lot worse than it did. And there was Larkin breaking his chops and that freak of a ride operator trying to creep him out. But the day had turned out okay. Cracking the ticket booth had gone smoother than he could've hoped for, and for the first time in a couple of months he had some real money in his pocket. Maybe all this good fortune would carry over to the blonde. It was worth going for.

The blonde glanced his way but he could see that she didn't see him; she was just looking in his general direction. But maybe that was a sign. She'd see him later, he'd make sure of it.

The waitress brought the two girls their food just as he and Stevie finished up their meal. A minute later, their waitress dropped their check down in front of Marty.

"Hang on a second," Marty told the waitress. "You want another beer, Stevie?"

"I thought we were done," Stevie said, confused again.

"I feel like another beer," Marty told the waitress.

"Yeah, okay, bring me another one, too," Stevie said.

The waitress picked up the check and hurried off.

"I thought we were done," Stevie repeated.

"I feel like hanging here a while longer," Marty said, his eyes on the blonde again.

"Why don't you just go over and talk to her?" Stevie asked.

"I'll talk to her when the time's right," Marty assured him.

The waitress brought their beers and the revised check.

Stevie picked up his glass as if it were an obligation. Marty relaxed and leaned back in his chair, sipping slowly at his beer while he watched the two girls eat their dinner.

When the girls called for their check, Marty put cash on the table for their bill.

"You treating?" Stevie asked.

"No. You can pay me later."

The girls gathered their things and made their way towards the exit.

Marty got up from his chair and followed them.

"What're we doing now?" Stevie asked, catching up to him.

"Let's see what the girls are gonna do," Marty responded.

"We're gonna follow them?"

"Kind of."

"So you can find a good time to talk to them?" Stevie persisted.

"Yeah, so I can talk to them."

CHAPTER THIRTEEN
LOVE HURTS

The first ride the blonde and her Latina friend visited after leaving the restaurant was the Tilt-a-Whirl, the clam shell backs of its cars following the park's ocean theme. Marty followed them there, being careful to hang back far enough not to be noticed. Stevie followed behind by a few paces, his lagging a show of his reluctance.

Marty, feeling better than he'd felt in a long time, watched the blonde slide across the car bench to make room for her friend. He could hear her laughter as the ride went into motion.

"We getting on?" Stevie asked.

"Are you kidding?" Marty asked. "We just ate."

"Oh," Stevie sounded bored.

"You don't have to stick with me," Marty said. "Take off and do whatever you want if you like. We can meet up later."

Stevie shifted his weight from foot to foot, his hands in his pockets.

"I wanna stick with you," Stevie said.

"Okay, then, what's the problem?" Marty asked.

"I don't know. Why don't you just go up and talk to them?" Stevie asked. "Following them around seems kinda weird."

"Whatta you mean by that?" Marty responded with a frown.

"Nothing. Nothing, Marty," Stevie answered, his nerves showing.

"I just think you should go up to them if you want to meet her. That's all."

Marty got his anger under control. He wouldn't let this pill popper ruin his mood tonight.

"I'll talk to them," he said. "When I see it's the right time, I'll talk to them."

Three minutes later, the Tilt-a-Whirl slowed and the girls' car stopped at the exit platform. They hurried down the ramp and away through the crowd, heading towards the park's second roller coaster, an almost exact twin of the one built at the end of the pier.

The blonde and her friend got into line for the coaster. Marty let a few people join the line behind the girls and then fell in behind them with Stevie on his heels. The clatter of the cars on the track and the screams of the riders echoed off the buildings and the smooth surface of the parking lot on the opposite side of the coaster.

"I love coasters," Stevie announced with the enthusiasm of a little kid.

"Yeah, they're a blast," Marty responded.

Three cars made up each train, and each car carried twelve riders, so the line moved quickly. In just a few minutes, they were climbing the lift hill. Stevie was taking in the view as they climbed higher and higher, but Marty's eyes were on the blonde riding three seats in front of him.

He felt excited being so close to her, and then there was the added juice in how he felt because she didn't even know he was there. He could watch her, but she couldn't see him.

Their car crested the lift hill and Marty watched the blonde's tan arms shoot into the air. There was a tattoo on her upper left arm, a lightning bolt zapping through a rose. She was his kind of girl. The coaster plummeted downward with a tremendous rush of wind. The riders screamed in happy terror as they raced along the rails, dropping, and then dropping again. After a last hill climb and a severe drop into a circle loop, the train coasted back into the station.

"That was great," Stevie laughed as they stepped onto the platform.

Marty didn't bother agreeing. He was busy keeping his eyes on the blonde and her friend as they climbed out of their car and headed back into the park. They took their time, looking at the sights as they maneuvered through the crowd. After a couple of minutes, they paused and appeared to exchange a few words, and then picked up their pace, heading towards the bumper cars.

"Hurry up, Stevie," Marty said, afraid he might lose sight of them.

"If they ride the bumper cars, we can get on, too, and crash into them," Stevie said. "That'd be a blast."

"Yeah," Marty muttered.

As he processed the idea, it didn't sound too bad. Bumper cars were all about getting a laugh by ramming into somebody. It'd get him close to the blonde and her friend, and they could share a few laughs on the ride when they rammed into each other. Afterwards, he'd have an opening to talk to them, talk to the blonde.

The girls reached the bumper cars, but continued past the entrance, heading around to the opposite side of the ride. Marty started getting a weird feeling. There was something familiar about this route and he didn't like it. In another few moments, he remembered why.

The girls were heading towards the Inferno Ghost Train, the dark ride. He could see that freak of a ride operator, Mr. Sabnock or whatever he said his name was, ushering riders into the cars with glee and dispatching them into the dark tunnel.

"I guess we're not riding this one with them," Stevie quipped.

"You want to lose some teeth?" Marty snapped at him.

"I didn't mean anything," Stevie answered.

Marty let it go and watched the girls get into the line for the dark ride. He made his way closer to the ride as the blonde and her friend progressed through the line. In a few minutes, they were at the front, ready to board the next car. They didn't have long to wait.

As the ride operator ushered the two girls into the car, he looked up at Marty and smiled. He didn't look around first, he didn't look up and just happen to see him. No, he knew exactly where to set his eyes when he looked up. And that stinking smile, it jeered and condemned. It was like being poked with a stick, and nobody was going to poke Marty Wedlow with a stick.

Without looking away, the ride operator punched a button on the control console and the car carried the girls into the tunnel. The moment they were out of sight, Marty advanced towards the ride. He could hear Stevie's footsteps trying to keep up behind him.

"What's your problem, asshole?" Marty called out, stopping at the restraining rail closest to the ride operator.

Sabnock's smile became more mocking as he continued ushering riders into the cars and seeing them off.

"Are you back for another ride?" Sabnock asked.

"I wanna know what your problem is," Marty replied, his voice angry.

"Marty, come on, let's go," Stevie said, his tone nervous.

"Get in line, Mr. Wedlow. You certainly must want to ride," Sabnock said. "After all, what you're sniffing after is inside, isn't it?"

And then he laughed. A low, raspy, gnawing laugh that made Marty angrier than he'd been in months.

"I'll slap that grin right off..." Marty growled as he began climbing over the rail.

He could feel Stevie pulling him back, pulling him off the rail.

"No, Marty, no!" Stevie pleaded.

Sabnock's laughter increased. Marty spun around and pushed Stevie up against the wall, ready to pound him.

"Think of the money," Stevie said in an intense whisper. "Think of the money. We get into any trouble now, we might lose the money. We might even get caught."

Marty let go of him. He was right. Without looking back at Sabnock, Marty walked past the small crowd that had frozen their own lives in the hopes of witnessing some violence.

"It's okay, everybody," Stevie said from behind him. "No worries, just a little misunderstanding."

And then came the ugly, hollow voice of Sabnock, slicing through the noise of the park like a knife. "See you again soon, Mr. Wedlow. See you again soon."

Marty retreated to the edge of the bumper cars and positioned himself where he could see the exit of the dark ride. He was already calming down. Stevie's surprising logic had helped with that. And when the blonde and her friend reappeared from the ride and walked through the exit, he felt a lot better. Seeing her again rekindled his excitement.

The girls made their way back to the pier where they headed for the Banana Train ride. They got in line, and again Marty let a few riders get between them before joining the line with Stevie. He was closer to them this time and he heard the blonde's friend call her 'Carrie.' He liked the sound of it. Yeah, *Carrie* was a nice name.

Once they'd ridden the Banana Train, the girls headed to the end of the pier and got in line for the roller coaster there. Stevie was jazzed to get another coaster ride into the day. As for Marty, he was feeling excited that he was becoming more comfortable around the girls.

The pier coaster shook up his senses. The speed of the ride colliding with the cool air blowing in from the sea was exhilarating. As he followed the girls off the ride, he again felt a new energy in him, a new confidence.

The girls stepped to the side of the thoroughfare, stopping to talk. They're figuring out what they're gonna do next, Marty thought. And then the Latina girl noticed him and Stevie standing there. She said something to the blonde, and then the blonde looked. The blonde looked right at him, her big, blue eyes taking him in from head to toe. She turned back to her friend. They exchanged a few words, and then began walking again, giggling together as they went.

"They made us," Stevie said, a little dismayed.

"Nah, this is what's supposed to happen," Marty reassured him.

It was what he'd been waiting for. He'd connected with her. Now it'd be easy to approach her, strike up a conversation.

The girls moved along the pier, heading back towards the shore. At the pier's halfway point, they veered off to the side and sat down on a bench next to the observation railing. Marty scanned the area and found what he was looking for. It was perfect.

With Stevie following along, Marty stepped up to the ice cream stand.

"Yeah, three double cones," Marty told the guy manning the concession. "One chocolate, one strawberry, one vanilla."

"You got it," the ice cream guy responded.

"You want an ice cream?" Marty asked Stevie.

Stevie shook his head. "I'm lactose intolerant. Gives me bad gas."

"Can you put 'em in one of those boxes?" Marty asked the ice cream guy as he put the second scoop on the first cone.

The guy nodded, slipping the cone into one of the four holes in the top of the carrying box that held it upright. Marty glanced back at the girls, making sure they were still on the bench. The Latina girl was lighting a cigarette.

"$9.75," the ice cream guy said, placing the last cone in the box.

"$9.75," Marty repeated, irritated. "Is this some kind of rare ice cream or something?"

The ice cream guy just shrugged as he took the money.

"Wait here," Marty instructed Stevie.

Doing his best to look casual and confident, Marty carried the box of ice cream cones over to the bench. The girls were chatting and laughing as he approached, and when he was within about ten feet of them, they both noticed him.

"Hi," he greeted them, stepping up beside the bench.

They exchanged a quick glance and looked up at him with thin, apprehensive smiles.

"What's up?" the Latina girl said.

"Not much. I noticed you over at the roller coaster," Marty told them.

"Yeah, we saw you there," the Latina girl responded, taking a puff on her cigarette.

He was glad the blonde wasn't smoking. Carrie, her friend had called her. He didn't like girls who smoked.

"And then I saw you sitting here, and I said to myself, those ladies look like they could use some ice cream."

They exchanged another glance and he could see they were smiling. He could see they were trying not to smile bigger than they were. He was getting to them.

"Yeah, thanks anyway," Carrie answered, her voice as sexy as he'd imagined it.

"We got chocolate. We got strawberry. We got vanilla," Marty said. "All the best flavors."

"My mom told me never to take sweets from strangers," the Latina girl said.

"I'm Marty. See, no problem, now we're not strangers."

The girls were looking at each other again, the same smiles on their lips, their eyes twinkling with some kind of private, chic communication.

"Come on," Marty urged. "It's just no-strings-attached ice cream. If you don't accept, then I'm gonna have to eat all of them myself. You don't want me getting sick, do you?"

Carrie looked at her friend. "Free ice cream. What the hell," she said.

He sat down on the bench next to the blonde and extended the box of cones.

"Which one do you want?" the blonde asked her friend.

"Vanilla," her friend answered, reaching for the cone.

"Sweet, 'cause I wanted the strawberry," Carrie said, lifting the cone from the box.

"That gives me the chocolate," Marty said. "My favorite."

He could feel the warmth of Carrie's body next to him. He watched her licking her cone, her pink tongue flicking across the ice cream, sucking thin layers of the treat into her mouth.

"Whatta you think? Good, huh?" Marty asked.

"Yeah, thanks," the Latina girl said.

"Thanks," Carrie echoed. She looked him over again. "So whatta you doing at Oceanside Park?"

"What am I doing?" Marty responded. "I'm hanging out with you right now."

"You don't seem like the amusement park kind of guy?" Carrie observed.

"What kind of guy am I, then?"

"Good question," Carrie muttered, returning her attention to the strawberry ice cream.

"Hey, I'm all about the fun here," Marty said, making sure he sounded charming, and licking away some melting ice cream before it became a mess. "The rides, games, the food, the beautiful women."

Carrie and her friend exchanged one of those glances again.

"Hey, I told you my name, but you didn't tell me yours," Marty pushed a little.

The girls suddenly seemed very focused on their ice cream cones.

"No, we didn't, did we?" Carrie giggled.

Her friend giggled along with her. It bugged him a little, but he let it go. The giggling didn't last long, and then they all focused on their ice cream in silence for a while.

"So what's up next?" he asked. "I mean, when you finish your ice cream."

"Hard to say," Carrie said, not bothering to look at him. "We just take it all as it comes."

"Might be fun if we all hang out for a while," Marty suggested.

"You think so?" the Latina girl asked.

Marty shrugged and shot her his most charming smile.

"You think so?" the Latina girl smiled at her friend.

"Big fun," Carrie answered.

Marty thought he heard a little smartass in the girl's tone, and when both of them shared one of their exclusive giggles, he was sure of it.

"Hey, I'm just suggesting," he told them, trying to disguise how offended he felt.

"Yeah, I know what you're suggesting," Carrie said with a jaded laugh. "You like 'em young, huh?"

"Carrie!" her friend laughed, her discomfort obvious.

"I don't see what the big deal is," Marty answered.

"Get some glasses," Carrie quipped.

She stood up from the bench and her friend with her.

"You're not leaving already?" Marty asked, rising with them.

"Oh, yeah," the Latina girl said, finishing the last bite of her cone.

"Come on, I just thought we could hang out the rest of the night, have some fun," he told them.

"Yeah?" Carrie responded. "Why'd you think that?"

The girls turned and walked away. He heard the giggling begin again and watched as Carrie tossed what remained of her ice cream cone into a nearby trash can. They'd been playing him. He felt his gut wrench as the anger and resentment roiled inside him. It was their loss, he told himself. It was their loss.

CHAPTER FOURTEEN
OPPORTUNITY KNOCKS

Marty finished his third beer of the day and gazed blankly into the thinning crowd of park goers. It was shortly after midnight and Oceanside Park was closing down attractions to get everybody out by the 1:00 AM closing time.

"I hate to see you feeling bad just 'cause those two girls blew you off," Stevie said with genuine sympathy.

"They didn't blow me off," Marty snapped. "They just had to go, that's all."

"You've been kind of moping around since they left, so I just thought you might be feeling bad," Stevie said.

"I've got nothing to feel bad about," he lied. "I've never had any problem getting a woman, and there's plenty of them out there."

It was over two hours since the two girls had shut him down and it had been eating at him ever since. After wandering the park for more time than he cared to admit, he finally planted himself on a stool at the Bavarian Beer Garden, which was nothing more than a patio facing the sea equipped with umbrellas and a few potted plants. He ordered a beer and had made it last for an hour. Stevie didn't want any alcohol and ordered a Pepsi instead, and even that irritated him.

The waitress dropped a check in front of him and hurried away without asking them if there'd be anything else.

"Everybody's in a big hurry to get home," Marty groused.

"I wouldn't mind leaving," Stevie said, slipping another pill out of his bottle and popping it in his mouth. "Long day."

"All right," Marty said, placing a few bills on the check and sliding off the stool.

They left the beer joint and strolled through the park towards the exit, blending in with all the other idiots who'd decided to close down the place. Only a few hours ago Marty had felt like he owned Oceanside Park, but now all he could think about was how he'd blown it again.

His gut was knotted with frustration. He'd let the blonde distract him, and if that wasn't enough, she'd played him, leading him on and then just walking away. Marty could still hear her giggling about it, laughing at him as she left him standing there alone on the pier.

He was mad, mad at himself. Mad he'd let himself get derailed by the girl. He pissed the whole night away. Instead of searching for more easy marks, he spent the time nursing his wounds, distracted by how the blonde had dissed him.

"The money," Marty said to himself.

"What?" Stevie asked.

"We've gotta get the money before we leave."

"Whoa," Stevie said. "I almost forgot."

"We'll get it now," Marty told him.

"What if the police are still watching the exit?" Stevie asked.

"Then I'll figure something out, but I'm not leaving it," Marty assured him.

They changed their direction, heading back towards the kids' ride with the oversized flower pots. They hadn't gone very far when Marty paused. About twenty feet in front of him were the two girls. They were standing still, their eyes fixed ahead of them.

Stevie followed his gaze and saw the girls.

"Come on, Marty," he said. "Let's just keep going."

But Marty couldn't keep going. He couldn't explain it, but that blonde, Carrie, he just had to stand there and watch her.

"Marty, come on," Stevie repeated.

"Just a minute," he said.

He shifted his position and he finally saw what they were looking at.

Moving through the diminishing crowd came a big Latino guy in a tee shirt and jeans. His muscular arms were tatted up and he was staring straight at Carrie's friend. She began fidgeting as he drew closer.

Marty spotted a closed souvenir stand only a few feet from the girls and headed for it.

"Where're you going?" Stevie asked, his tone anxious.

"Shut up," Marty answered.

Stevie reluctantly trailed behind him and in a few seconds they were concealed behind the little stand, both of them doing their best to look like they were just hanging out, perhaps waiting for someone. Marty couldn't risk poking his head around to watch the scene. They were too close, but he could hear well enough.

"What're you doing here?" the Latina girl said, making it sound like more of a challenge than a question.

"Looking for you," the guy responded. "I been looking for you all day."

"You got a lot of nerve comin' here. I saw you with that girl," the Latina girl said.

"Ah, come on, Angela, please," the guy pleaded.

So that was her name.

"Can't we just talk?" the guy asked.

"Why don't you go talk to her?" Angela hissed at him.

"It's not what you think," the guy almost whined.

"I'll bet it is," Carrie chuckled.

Marty didn't hear the guy say anything to that remark. A good choice.

"How'd you find me, anyway?" Angela asked him.

"I went by Carrie's house. Carrie's mom told me where to find you before she slammed the door in my face."

"Too bad she didn't slam it on your dick," Angela responded.

Marty could hear Carrie laugh at the remark.

"You're mad, I get it," the guy said. "You got a reason to be mad."

There was silence now. The remark must have surprised the Angela girl.

"You really hurt me."

"I know. And I'm sorry," the guy said, working it. "I love you and I'd never wanna do anything to hurt you."

"It's better you just get lost," Angela told him.

She still sounded angry, but Marty thought the 'I love you' must have thrown a little water on the fire.

"Look, I was stupid," the guy admitted. "I made a stupid mistake."

"What? You want me to argue?" Angela sounded snappish again.

"Come on, let's just talk. Let's get a little food or something and we'll talk," the guy pushed.

"I wouldn't want your new girlfriend getting all jealous on you," Angela said.

"She's nothing. I swear she's nothing," the guy answered. "Come on, at least let me explain."

"That should be good," Carrie chuckled again.

"Would you just shut it, Carrie?" the guy said, sounding frustrated. "Angela, please. You're so beautiful and I miss you, and I feel like shit about all of it. Let's talk, you know, somewhere in private."

Marty imagined the guy glancing at Carrie when he said that.

"Talk about what?" Angela asked, sounding less reluctant.

"About how stupid I am," the guy answered. "We'll talk about how stupid I am and what a shitty mistake I made. And if it doesn't satisfy you, then I'll leave you alone. I'll leave you alone if that's what you want."

"I don't know," Angela said, her resolve weakening. "What do you think?"

Marty knew she'd get around to asking Carrie.

"Your call," Carrie said.

"Even if I want to, I can't go," Angela said. "We came together. I can't leave Carrie here alone."

"You're okay with it, aren't you, Carrie?" the guy asked.

"I'm not leaving you," Angela said before Carrie could answer.

The conversation stalled for several seconds.

"If you want to go with him, I'll be fine," Carrie said.

"You sure?" Angela asked, sounding relieved.

"Yeah, if you want to go talk, go talk," Carrie assured her. "I'm just going to my car and going home, anyway."

"As long as you're sure," Angela said.

"Call me tomorrow," Carrie told her.

Marty could hear footsteps moving away and risked taking a cautious look. Angela and the guy were moving away.

"Angela," Carrie called out.

Marty pulled back behind the concession stand.

"Make sure your bullshit detector's set on high," Carrie said.

He heard the footsteps again and again risked moving to the edge of the wall to look.

The reunited couple was already being swallowed up in the throng of people heading for the exit. Carrie, her back to him, stood watching them go. She rummaged in her handbag for something and then began walking towards the exit.

Marty slipped out from behind the stand and followed her. Stevie was at his side, tugging at his arm.

"Where are you going?" Stevie asked, his tone unhappy, already knowing the answer.

"Wherever she's going," Marty told him.

"Marty, no. Why?" Stevie asked.

"We never got to know each other. But we're gonna."

CHAPTER FIFTEEN
A LITTLE STALKING

He had to be more careful than earlier in the evening. There weren't as many people to obscure him from view, and he wasn't about to let Carrie see him.

"I don't think this is a good idea," Stevie whined.

"What's not a good idea?"

"Whatever you're thinking about this girl," Stevie replied.

"You know where the money is, right?" Marty asked him, keeping his eyes on the girl some thirty feet ahead.

"Sure I do," Stevie responded.

"You go get it. Make sure nobody sees you," Marty instructed.

Marty reached into his pants pocket and retrieved his key ring. He slipped off his room key and pushed it into Stevie's palm.

"Get the money. Take the bus and go straight back to my place. You wait for me there," Marty told him.

"Let's both go get it together," Stevie suggested.

"You wait for me there," Marty repeated. "And I'm warning you, Stevie, you even think about opening that bag before I get back and I'll beat you to death. Understand?"

"Yeah, sure, Marty," Stevie said.

"Get going."

Stevie dropped behind him, and Marty glanced back to see him heading in the right direction. But Marty felt a wave of doubt cascade over him. He'd let this blonde get inside his head again and he didn't even realize it was happening. What was he thinking? He'd trust nobody with any of his money and he just sent that little pill popper to get more of it than he'd scored in months.

There was a break in the crowd ahead of him and he had a clear, but brief view of the blonde. Her long, tanned legs carried her gracefully along, that sweet little ass swaying side to side in a perfect, irresistible rhythm. He had a final, fleeting thought about the money, but then it was gone. He couldn't take his eyes off the girl.

She weaved her way through the tired park goers, heading for the exit with everyone else. He stayed with her, doing his best to keep a few bodies between him and the girl in case she had some reason to look back towards him. But she didn't. She reached the exit, pushed through the turnstile and headed out towards the big parking lot on the north side of the park.

Marty passed through the turnstile and the few security people still hanging around didn't look twice at him. It looked like they'd given up searching purses and bags, too. Good, Stevie wouldn't have any trouble getting the money out.

Marty reached the edge of the parking lot and stopped in his tracks. There were still quite a few cars in the lot and he somehow had lost sight of her. A swell of panic overtook him, but it was short-lived. There she was, emerging from the shadows about sixty feet in front of him, making her way through the parked cars.

She kept walking deeper into the lot. She must have gotten to the park late, Marty reasoned, and the entrance side of the lot was already full. Nearby a tired looking guy and his tired looking wife jammed their kids into a minivan. The engine turned over and they backed out of their space.

Fewer cars occupied this section of the lot. He noticed Carrie move the purse hanging against her side around to her front. The faint sound of jingling keys reached him. She must be drawing closer to her car. On either side of him, couples climbed into their cars and started the engines. The moving headlights rippled across the cars pushing shadows ahead of them.

Marty scanned the area and saw no one else in the shadows. It looked like it was just him and the girl now. He began walking faster, closing the distance between them. If he didn't catch up to her by the time she reached the car, all this effort would be for nothing.

He heard his own footsteps against the blacktop of the parking lot, and so did she. Marty noticed her glance casually back over her shoulder. He was certain she had seen him because now she was moving faster. She was afraid. Good, he thought. She deserves to be afraid after the way she dissed him. He increased his speed and saw that he was moving closer to her.

The girl glanced back again and then broke into a full run. He began running, never taking his eyes off her as she weaved between the few cars left at this end of the lot. She stopped beside the driver's side of an older model, beat up Chevy Malibu, almost slamming into it.

He could see her chest heaving as he approached, drawing deep, panicked breaths. She was fumbling with the keys, rushing to get the car key into the lock. She must have seen him out of the corner of her eye as he rushed up to the rear of the car, because her head jerked upward for a split second. In her panic, she dropped the keys.

He paused at the rear of the car, looking at her. She quivered with fear, her eyes wide with apprehension and recognition. Her body bent forward and her fingers opened, but he could see she was torn between bending over to pick up the keys or keeping her eyes on him. She decided on the keys and kneeled down.

"No," he said, his tone sharp.

She froze and then straightened up again, her eyes wider and her lips pressed together. He closed the distance between them.

"I'll get them," he said.

He bent down and grabbed the keys. As he straightened up, he had a vague sense of the girl pulling her hand from inside the purse. She raised her arm and he glimpsed the little can in her hand. Marty realized it was pepper spray just as she jammed her thumb down on the nozzle button.

He jerked his head away and threw his arm over his face, but he wasn't quite fast enough. Marty felt the cool spray cover the left side of his face, and then the coolness was gone, replaced by a painful burning on his skin and in his left eye. He roared in pain and blindly reached out for her.

The girl tried to retreat, but she wasn't fast enough. He grabbed hold of her arm wielding the pepper spray and wrenched at it. She tried to twist away, but he tightened his grip and yanked her up against him. The girl fought hard, and as he pushed her up against the car, she screamed at the top of her lungs. He heard the can of spray clatter against the ground and then he felt the girl's fist smash hard into his cheek.

He bellowed with pain, and as he brought his free hand up to his face, he felt the girl twist hard out of his grasp and push away from him. Her running footsteps echoed around him and with his good eye, he saw her sprinting towards the far end of the parking lot.

He glanced around to see if anyone was coming in answer to the scream, but saw no one. The noise still coming from the park probably covered the sound. He caught sight of her again, moving fast, a sliver of light reflecting off her blonde hair. Furious, he followed her into the shadows.

CHAPTER SIXTEEN
PURSUIT

S he was heading towards the corner of the lot, and that was fine by him. It was darker there and the chain-link fence that surrounded the lot was ten feet high. She'd have nowhere to go, and he'd make sure the bitch didn't get far.

He saw her reach the fence. She paused only a moment before moving again. His left eye was burning like crazy. He felt the tears running down his face, and he was having trouble seeing with just one eye. Through the darkness, for a moment, it looked like she was on the opposite side of the fence. He tried to focus harder as he ran towards her and then realized she really was on the opposite side of the chain-link. She had gotten out of the parking lot somehow and disappeared into the shadows as he watched.

He reached the area of fence where he last saw her and moved along down the fence. Near the very corner of the lot he saw it, a tear in the chain-link. Hurrying to the spot, he thought it looked as if someone had taken cutters to the heavy wire in order to create a movable flap. Maybe somebody had been looking at breaking into the parked cars. On the opposite side of the fence, he could see a row of loading docks and several semitrailers parked in the dock spaces.

He pushed the fencing aside and ducked through the opening. Somewhere in the darkness ahead of him, something clattered on the pavement. Following the sound, he began running.

Up ahead he saw a dim glow on the ground. Reaching the spot, he saw it was a cell phone, its screen cracked. The girl had tried getting it out of her purse while she ran, fumbled and dropped it.

Marty stuffed the phone in his pocket and continued forward, breaking into a full run. He rounded a corner at the end of the dock row. Up ahead were more warehouses and more loading platforms. He peered into the darkness and saw her running hard. It surprised him he was closer to her than originally thought. He put on more speed.

She heard his approaching footsteps and looked back over her shoulder, almost stumbling as she did so. Seeing him, she began sobbing and he could hear little cries coming from her.

He was within twenty feet of her now and when she sensed his nearness she let out a wailing scream. He closed the distance in seconds and grabbed hold of her, wrapping his arms around her from behind.

"Nooooo," she screamed.

He clamped a hand over her mouth as she struggled and twisted, trying to get away. Not this time, he thought. This time, little Carrie would get what she deserved.

He spotted a trailer parked at the end of the dock next to them, its back door open to the shadows within. It was perfect, Marty thought as he dragged her up the nearby steps to the loading platform. He practically had to carry her, and her constant twisting and turning didn't make it easy. He dragged her along the platform to the back of the trailer and pulled her inside. Now she'd learn that it wasn't a smart idea to mess with him.

CHAPTER SEVENTEEN
A FAINT SCREAM

"It didn't take Baumgarten long to put the finger on Wedlow," Romero said, guiding the cruiser through Oceanside Park's parking lot entrance.

"He was certain, that's for sure," Larkin responded. He was riding shotgun and already scanning the people on the sidewalk and looking hard at the cars leaving the parking lot for any sign of Martin Wedlow.

"Pull in over there," Larkin pointed. "The restricted zone next to the entrance."

"Got it," Romero responded.

Romero pulled to the curb and cut the engine. Larkin grabbed several copies of the six-pack page with Wedlow's photo on it and climbed out of the car. Romero was right behind him.

"What's the plan?" Romero asked.

"We show his photo to the security guys at the gate and tell them to keep an eye out," Larkin said. "Then we'll make our way into the park and see if we can spot him."

Romero nodded, and they began walking towards the main entrance. They hadn't gone far when Larkin thought he heard something. It was faint and distant, but he thought it sounded like a scream, a woman's scream. He stopped and listened.

"What?" Romero asked, tired.

"I thought I heard a scream."

"People on the rides in the park," Romero theorized.

"It wasn't like that," Larkin said, looking back towards the parking lot. "It came from out there."

He hurried back to the cruiser, pulled open the driver's side door, and stepped up on the frame. He looked out over the parking lot, moving his eyes from section to section. And then he saw the two figures, just shadows moving through the night. He could just make them out, small glimmers of light reflecting off skin and hair as they cut through the shadows. Somebody was running like hell towards the far corner of the lot and there was another somebody running after them.

"Move it!" Larkin called out.

Romero ran back to the car and around to the passenger side. He jumped in as Larkin slid behind the wheel and turned over the engine.

"What'd you see?" Romero asked, leaning forward and switching on the flashing emergency lights.

"Somebody's being chased down out there, at the corner of the lot," Larkin asked.

Romero got on the radio and called it in as Larkin hit the gas.

Larkin tapped the cruiser horn to stop a pickup truck in the process of backing out of its parking space. He swerved around the rear of the truck and pushed down on the accelerator. Reaching the far side of the lot, he turned into the far lane and followed the chain-link fence towards the beach.

Romero switched on the car mount floodlight and swept it back and forth between the interior of the parking lot to the fence.

"You see anything?" Larkin asked. "Damn it! Where are they?"

"Nothing yet," Romero reported.

"I'd swear they were over here somewhere," Larkin said, frustrated.

They were almost at the end of the lot when Romero moved the floodlight back to the fence.

"There," he called out.

Larkin stopped the cruiser. Romero focused the light on a flap cut in the chain-link. They got out of the car and hurried to the fence.

Larkin kneeled down next to the opening and moved the beam of his flashlight over the fence. He moved the beam into the property on the other side of the chain-link, sweeping it through the darkness. And then he heard it, the sound of running footsteps reflecting off the concrete and warehouse buildings.

"*That* I heard," Romero said.

Larkin pushed at the torn section of fencing and eased through the opening. Romero followed him through while he held up the flap. Switching on their flashlights, they hurried towards the row of loading docks.

Larkin listened intently as they made their way through the shadows, but heard nothing. The facility was big, it was dark, and there were too damn many places somebody could hide. He didn't like the situation, nor that he'd already lost the trail.

A metallic, hollow clatter reached them through the darkness.

"Best guess that way," Larkin pointed.

Following their flashlight beams, they hurried forward into the shadows.

CHAPTER EIGHTEEN
ATTACK

M arty tried to get his hand on the knife he'd lifted in the alley as he dragged the girl towards the rear of the empty trailer, but she wouldn't stop struggling. Now she began twisting and kicking with a renewed, fright-fueled energy. She landed a couple of solid kicks to his shins, but the pain was nowhere near enough to stop him.

She twisted and slipped out of his grasp, but only for a moment. Mary grabbed hold of her arm before she traveled five feet and yanked her back. He spun her against the wall of the trailer. The girl's back connected hard with the metal and it stunned her.

Marty was on her, pushing his body against hers, pinning her against the wall. He tried to kiss her, but she jerked her head to the side. Her desperate struggling excited him even more. Without warning, he dropped his hand downward, grabbing her between her legs.

Marty pulled her away from the wall and tried to force her to the floor.

"No," she groaned.

She fought harder now, harder than she had before, and somehow pulled away from him again. She rushed forward, but he jumped at her, and taking hold of her, began pushing her downward again. The girl kept up the fight, but when his fist slammed into her cheek, it slowed her down good.

The girl dropped to the floor of the trailer. He was on her again, straddling her, his weight pinning her under him. She flailed at him, but he pushed her arms aside and ripped open her blouse. He moved his hands between her legs again, fumbling with the buttons of her shorts. She screamed at the top of her lungs.

He clamped a hand down over her mouth, staring down at her, furious. He was pushing hard and he could see she couldn't breathe. And then he heard the voices.

"Did you hear it?" a man's voice filtered into the back of the trailer.

"That way!" another voice responded.

Marty froze and looked back towards the door. Turning back to the girl, he lowered his mouth to her ear.

"You make a sound when I let go of you, I swear I'll turn around and kick your brains out right here," he promised her.

She stared up at him, paralyzed with fear.

"Understand?" he hissed, cuffing her on the side of her head.

She nodded.

In an instant, he was on his feet, and with a last look down at her, he hurried to the trailer door. Hugging the wall beside the door, he took a cautious look outside, then slipped into the darkness.

CHAPTER NINETEEN
BEGINNING OF THE END

The scream bounced off the warehouse walls, making the source difficult to locate. Knowing they were close, Larkin and Romero pulled their guns, swept their flashlight beams ahead of them and increased their pace.

About a hundred feet ahead was another semitrailer backed up against the end of the loading dock, its doors hanging open. Their flashlight beams revealed nothing in the opening, but disappearing over the far side of the loading dock was a man.

"Oscar!" Larkin shouted.

"Saw him," Romero confirmed as they both broke into a run.

As they approached the truck, they saw a pale figure emerging from the darkness of the trailer. They spread out and leveled their guns at the figure.

"Police," Larkin called out.

A blond girl, her clothing torn, stumbled out of the trailer onto the dock. Seeing them, she began sobbing and collapsed on the platform.

"I've got the girl," Romero yelled.

Romero called in their status on his vest radio as Larkin ran for the semitrailer. He ducked underneath, rushing to the opposite side. Hearing running footsteps ahead of him, he took off after them.

Rounding the corner at the edge of the loading dock, he found himself in a narrow alley between two buildings. Gooseneck lamps that had to be at least forty years old were mounted on the side of the building about every thirty feet. They cast a line of dim, circular pools of light along the passage. The figure of a man abruptly appeared in the pool at the end of the building, and then was gone again.

Larkin channeled his high school track days and put on as much speed as he had in him. The echoes of his footsteps merged with those of the man somewhere ahead of him. He reached the end of the building and listened. The footsteps reached him, coming from the right. He made the turn and put on the steam again. The sound of approaching sirens in the distance reached him.

Ahead of him was another row of loading docks, many of them with trailers backed up to them. There was something familiar about them and he realized this was the area he and Romero had entered after coming through the torn fence.

He saw his suspect ahead, illuminated by the warehouse lights. There was something familiar about him, something about the way he moved.

"Police," Larkin shouted. "Stop."

Larkin didn't expect the guy to stop and ran even harder after he shouted. He was closing the distance. The suspect changed his direction, and as he passed through another pool of light, turned to look over his shoulder.

"Son of a bitch," Larkin cursed.

It was Marty Wedlow and he was doubling back toward Oceanside Park.

CHAPTER TWENTY
DESPERATION

M arty darted into the middle of the driveway to avoid the lights on the side of the building. His heart pounded, almost beating out of his chest. He could tell by the footsteps in the blackness behind him that the cop was gaining. The wail of the approaching sirens couldn't even muffle them.

Marty pulled the knife from its sheath. There was no good reason for it, but the blade in his hand somehow calmed his fear.

A hundred feet ahead of him was the fence enclosing the parking lot. He just had to get back through the gap in the fence and head for his car, and he'd be golden. He weaved around the back of a parked trailer, almost losing his footing, but now he had a clear line to the fence.

Ninety feet, eighty feet, seventy feet, sixty feet. His chest heaved, fighting to draw in enough breath to keep going.

"Wedlow, stop!" he heard the voice scream behind him.

It had to be Larkin. The cop and his partner had been at the park that day and who else would know his name? Marty wasn't about to give that stinking cop the satisfaction and put on a fresh burst of speed. He'd be out of the city tomorrow, anyway. It wouldn't matter that Larkin spotted him.

He was almost at the fence now and headed for the torn section in the corner.

"Stop, Marty. Drop the knife," Larkin yelled from behind him. "Drop it! You're gonna get shot."

Marty threw the knife aside as he dived for the opening in the fence.

"Stop!" Larkin shouted again. "Get down, face down on the ground."

Shit! That crazy Larkin would shoot him. And all over some stupid blonde.

He pulled up the flap of chain-link and pushed through. A jagged piece of fencing caught on his pant leg and he went down hard in the parking lot. He tugged his pants free and got back on his feet.

He began running full speed towards his car parked in the middle of the lot. There were only a few cars left now, so he'd have little cover. He had to get to the car as quickly as possible.

The scream of the sirens grew louder as he ran for his car. And then three patrol cars sped into the parking lot, their emergency lights flashing, heading right for him. He'd never make the car now.

The nearest section of fence ran parallel to the inland roller coaster. It was his best bet now and he ran hard for it.

As he closed in on the opposite fence, Marty got a sudden feeling, a feeling that Larkin was falling behind. True or not, it spurred him forward.

The roller coaster structure towered over him now, the ambient light squeezing through the steel girders casting twisted shadows on the pavement below. He scoped out the fence as he approached. The top angled some sixteen inches outward over the parking lot, but at least there was no barbed wire on it. He'd have to try it. He had no choice.

Marty leaped upward as he reached the chain-link, fastening himself to it like a bug on a wall. He scrambled upward, fighting for footholds, the wire cutting into his palms and fingers. The sound of approaching patrol cars closing in on him echoed across the pavement. Marty took hold of the heavy wire with both hands and then swung his leg out and upward. He didn't make the height he needed. His leg fell back downward and he almost lost his grip. His desperation pushed him to try again, and this time he hooked his foot over the top of the overhang. Hearing the brakes of the patrol cars squealing to a stop, he catapulted his body over the top, hung on to the fence for a split second, and then dropped to the ground. He landed hard and felt a burst of sharp pain in his left ankle.

He headed under the roller coaster, weaving in and out of the steel columns. Stabs of pain accompanied each of the first few steps he took, but the adrenaline kept him pressing forward. The pain soon lessened to a deep throbbing, and even though he had to favor his left leg, he found he could run again. He reached the far side of the coaster, and exhausted, paused to catch his breath and get his bearings. He looked back from where he had just come.

Larkin was at the base of the fence holstering his pistol as two officers hurried out of one of the three police cruisers that screeched to a stop. Larkin began scrambling up the fence and the other two men followed close behind him. The other two cruisers gunned their engines, spun around and took off again, heading for the park's front entrance.

Marty took a deep breath and began running again, heading into the park. The two cruisers would be at the front of the park within seconds, and he was certain that more cops were already there. If he could get through to the pier before they caught up to him, he might be able to get away in the ocean. It was dark and they'd have a tougher time following him in the water.

With most of the colorful attraction lights off, replaced by sparse utility lighting, the park took on an eerie appearance. He ran through a black and gray world with twisted shadows that crawled along the ground and up the sides of the attractions. The sirens were cutting off now, but the last remnants of their screams reverberated across the empty grounds, and even when they stopped altogether, he could hear them still echoing through his head.

His ankle was killing him as he sprinted towards one of the park's main thoroughfares. He could hear multiple footsteps slapping against the pavement somewhere behind him, the panic gripping his chest increasing with the sound of every step. The thoroughfare housed a variety of game arcade and food concessions. The moment he set foot in it, he heard shouts from his left. Half a dozen cops were running towards him from the front of the park.

He turned in the ocean's direction, and at the first break in the line of buildings, bolted back into the shelter of the darkened thrill rides. The sound of pursuing footsteps seemed to be everywhere now, all around him. He paused, trying to decide on a path of escape, but everything looked twisted and jumbled to him. He ran blindly onward.

Marty had almost forgotten about the pepper spray, but now beads of sweat liquefied the chemical that had dried on his forehead and carried it down into his eyes. He wiped at them with his forearm as he ran, but it only made the burning worse.

The Tilt-a-Whirl came into view ahead of him and beyond that he could see the outline of the pier, still a full block away. He'd make it, he told himself, he'd get there ahead of them. But then three more cops appeared from somewhere behind the antique carousel, blocking the path to the pier. They spotted him and raced straight for him.

He spun around and headed along the side of the Tilt-a-Whirl. He was running blind now, panic and desperation tightening around his guts like a hungry python.

The bumper cars came into view ahead of him, the cars' dark silhouettes backlit by a strange and dim, red-orange glow coming from somewhere on the far side of the open ride enclosure. Footsteps, too close, pulled his attention. Larkin, gripping his pistol, was running straight towards him.

"Give it up, Marty," Larkin yelled.

Marty gasped for breath as he altered his course, running around the far side of the bumper cars. The glowing light drew him towards it, like a moth to a flame.

Nearing the far side of the bumper car structure, the dark ride he loathed came into view. The light was coming from it. The INFERNO GHOST TRAIN sign bathed in the reddish glow. The fake stone facade seemed to smolder under it, and the large demon head in the center archway glared down at him, its mouth gaping wide as to devour him. None of its cars were moving, but the ride looked as if it was still active.

The ride operator, Sabnock, emerged from the shadows beside the ride console, staring straight at him. The freak was beckoning to him, waving him over with his long, bony fingers. And as Marty drew closer he could see Sabnock was speaking to him.

"Hurry, Mr. Wedlow," the hollow voice reached him. "Hurry. It's your only way out."

Sabnock extended one of his long fingers and punched a button on the console. One of the empty cars rolled to a stop in front of him.

There was no way, Marty thought. He hated that ride, and there was no way.

"Wedlow!" Larkin's yell came from behind him.

Marty's fear and confusion stopped him in his tracks, and he looked back. The son of a bitch cop was close now, too close, running at him with that damn gun raised.

"You're out of choices, Mr. Wedlow," Sabnock's voice captured his attention again. "It's your only refuge now."

There was no other choice now, and Marty sprinted towards the dark ride as if he were trying to outrun the fear that was consuming him. Once he was inside, maybe he could find a way out. There must be an emergency exit or a service door somewhere inside the ride. He saw Sabnock's tight-lipped smile widen as he neared the ride. He vaulted over the restraining rail and threw himself into the waiting car.

"There was never a doubt you'd return to us," Sabnock said, leering down at him.

Sabnock laughed as he stretched one of his long fingers towards a large, green lighted button on the console. It was a laugh full of madness and hate. The finger depressed the button. Marty heard the electrical circuit snap closed and caught a brief glimpse of a small tongue of flame as the green light flashed to red.

The safety bar dropped into place and Marty gripped it in terror as the car lurched forward, crashed through the double entrance doors, and plunged into the darkened tunnel beyond. The rattling laughter followed him into the passage as the blackness closed in around him.

CHAPTER TWENTY-ONE
LAST RIDE

The blackness was complete, but Marty knew right away that something was different, something was wrong with the ride. The air was heavy, thick, and warm. It swirled and eddied around him, and he found it hard to breathe. And there was an odd smell, not strong but sure as hell unpleasant. They'd turned the air conditioning off; that was it, of course.

The car rattled and shook, and he couldn't be sure in the darkness, but it felt like it was moving fast. He regretted his choice. He didn't like these dark rides, his fear of them drilled deep. He regretted thinking that he could get away from Larkin and the rest of the cops this way. How stupid could he be?

A dim, reddish glow appeared through the blackness ahead of him, flickering as if it was fighting to penetrate a heavy fog. And then, with a horrible chill, he began feeling he was not alone in the darkness. He could feel it, a presence, as if someone else or *something* else was coming closer to him.

The strange, glowing light grew brighter ahead, focused on a gnarled, dead tree. A bloodcurdling scream jolted him so hard he jumped upward, only to be knocked back down by the safety bar that slammed into his upper thighs. A man, his hands tied behind his back, hurtled downward. The rope around his neck stretched taut and the hangman's knot tightened behind his left ear. The man uttered a final, strangled scream that sounded along with a sickening thud.

The body hung unmoving, rotating slowly at the end of the rope. As the face swung into view, Marty gasped.

It was Stevie, eyes bulging out from his head. His mouth was frozen open in a final, desperate gasp. The face and neck were already displaying an ugly, purple discoloration, and his head was cocked at a grotesque angle.

What the hell was this? Marty knew he must get out of this place. He tried to rise again, to squeeze out from under the safety bar. But the harder he struggled, the tighter the bar seemed to press in on him.

A cacophony of ghostly wails drew all his attention. Ahead were several phantom figures on either side of the track, their pale robes billowing around them in the hot, turbulent air. They fixed their dead eyes on him—staring, glaring, angry. They closed in on the car. Marty could hear them speaking. He was certain they were speaking. Low, unintelligible, but threatening words spewed forth from their gaping mouths and hung in the dense air.

They were all moving towards him, reaching for him, claws as sharp as knives swiping at him. Marty felt burning pains along his cheek, and then across his forehead. He was sweating from the heat and the fear, and the sweat seeped into the deep scratches, burning and stinging. He raised his arms, crossing them in front of his face for protection. Searing pain in each of his arms and chest followed the sound of ripping fabric. Marty heard himself scream.

He was finally past them, out of their reach, and the tunnel plunged into darkness once again. Marty felt like he was about to crawl out of his own skin. His mouth opened to cry for help, but all he heard was a pathetic whimpering, gurgling sound.

Once again, there was light coming from up ahead; a dim, red, flickering light. He recognized it from before, the cellophane flames lighted by red spotlights, and the pathetic dummies of the people burning in the fake fire.

But again, something was changing. The air was more stifling and carried the heat of a furnace. The flickering cellophane morphed into actual flames and the dummies into real, tortured people. They wailed and screamed as the fire swept up around them, unable to move within the conflagration. And even though the flames touched them, melted skin and charred them, none of the bodies perished.

The car plunged into the flames and he screamed crazily as he felt his skin blister under the heat of the fire. He thrashed and kicked in his tiny, moving prison, pushing hard at the restraining bar that only burned his hands in the effort. The heat took the last of his hope and he collapsed back in the seat to wait for the flames to take him.

He wondered if he had somehow lost his mind, that all of this was delusion. But the pain from his scorched skin and ugly scratches reminded him that this was all too real.

The wailing of the burning souls faded away and the tortured, scarred bodies disappeared into the embers of the dying flames. Only a hazy, orange glow was left, barely visible through the blackness.

The air remained thick and hot and an unexpected quiet fell over the darkness. He could hear only the creaking of the car as it continued speeding forward. And then he glimpsed movement ahead and above him, a slight glimmer of silver-white catching some of the pitiful light. It was a long, curved strand of thread or some kind of fiber. It wasn't just a single thread. More of them came into view as he drew nearer.

He tasted bile in his mouth as he realized what it was. A web, it was a large web that floated in the blackness, and crawling downward on it was a large, black spider. He'd never seen a spider so large, except in books, and then he could only glimpse the photo a moment before being overwhelmed with revulsion.

The spider reached the edge of the web and then dropped off the side, dangling from a single strand of silk. Lower and lower it descended, and the closer it drew to the floor, the larger it grew.

Marty struggled and squirmed in the car's seat, frantic to shield himself from the eight-legged monster now coming for him. He heard a pathetic, crying scream in the air and then realized it was coming from him. He couldn't look at the thing nearing the floor on that glistening strand of web. The car was picking up speed. Maybe he'd get past the horrible thing before it reached the floor.

"God!" Marty cried out to the darkness. "Get me out of here. Please God, get me out of this and I swear I'll do anything you want."

The spider was grotesquely huge now, its bulbous body the size of a dog. It was almost to the floor, but the car shot past it. Marty twisted around in time to see it touch the floor and take after the car, scuttling forward, its huge mandibles opening and closing as it closed in.

Marty cried out again, his body weak with fear, the panic physically painful. And then a roar shook the car. He jerked around and his mouth opened in a silent scream. A sensation of deep anguish now coupled with his terror.

The Devil on the rock wall. At first it appeared as it had earlier in the day, the rubbery skin an ugly brownish gray, the flashing reptilian eyes. But then it leaned out from the wall, the rotted claws of its feet gripping the rock ledge while the huge dragon wings flapped in the searing air.

Marty could still hear the spider scuttling and chittering behind him, but now he couldn't move his eyes from what lay before him.

The Devil extended its right arm towards him, and he could see the claw-tipped fingers opening wide. Marty had called out to God for help, but he knew it was a worthless plea when he'd done it. He'd ignored God and God's ways his entire life, and now it was not God reaching for him, but Satan.

Marty braced himself for the sting of the razor-sharp claws, but the immense creature reached past him and scooped up the spider in an effortless sweep of his arm. As Marty watched in horror and revulsion, the Devil's mouth opened wide, a gaping chasm of rotting teeth and long fangs. It shoved the spider into its mouth and closed its fangs down on it, swallowing it whole.

The Devil glared at him until the car passed into the cavern opening below its perch on the rock wall.

Blackness squeezed in around him again and the sweltering air turned cold, chilling him to the bone. A soft, white light faded up from the darkness ahead of him and two figures appeared in the glow. He strained to see through the darkness and gasped with recognition.

Standing in the shadows was the old coot from the market. *Baumgarten*, Larkin had called him. And next to him was a kid, the clerk from the ticket booth he'd knocked over that evening. Their faces were bruised and cut, just the way he'd left them. They stared at him as the car carried him closer to them, their expressions displaying a strange, amused interest in him. The car shot past them, but their eyes stayed on him every moment.

His victims were barely out of sight when he heard crying up ahead. The sobbing was soft, but growing in volume, and echoed around him as if it would never stop. Up ahead, two girls came into view, each of them illuminated in a soft, warm light that shimmered around them. Who were they? They looked a little familiar, but he couldn't be sure.

As the car drew closer to them, he could see them better. One girl was half naked, her summer dress hanging on her slender body. Her face was swollen and bruised, and her thighs bruised as well. The other one was in the same shape, bruised and cut, her clothing torn. Both girls stared at him with empty eyes, their faces drenched in pain and grief.

He remembered now. Marty didn't know their names, but he'd come across them at a couple of parties, college parties, if he was remembering right. They'd come on to him, so he'd ended up banging them. Maybe it got rough, but so what? Why were they here? What was the big deal?

The car was almost on them now and the misery on their faces transformed into anger. No, not just anger. It was a hateful fury that he could feel. He shrank back in his seat in a futile attempt to shield himself from the intensity of it. The girls turned and followed the car as it raced past them. At least they'd never catch up to him at that speed, he thought.

The reverberations of the girls' crying sped along with the car and were joined by a pair of weak, pathetic screams. An elderly couple came into view in the car's path. Their faces were drawn in pain, sadness, and fear, and the ugly bruises on both of them reminded him of the time he'd needed a car. Old and frail, it had been a breeze taking it from them, but both of them had protested and he'd had to teach them a lesson.

But now there was a fierceness to the fear and pain in their faces as they reached out for him, trying to take hold of him with their long, clawlike fingers.

He could feel their fingernails scratch at him as the car moved past them, the sting of it as real and horrible as everything he'd been through since boarding this cursed ride. When two more figures faded up from the darkness, he was certain he couldn't take anymore.

He could see that they were two men. One of them was in uniform and, for a moment, he was certain the cops had gotten inside the ride from one of the maintenance doors and headed him off. But he soon saw that it wasn't a city cop, it was a sheriff in the typical khaki uniform. There was no mistaking this guy. It was the only time he'd ever hit anybody with a car. He thought he'd killed this sheriff, but here he was, coming towards him with a bad limp. With every step, there was a wince of pain on the man's face, and the glare of hatred grew more intense.

Staggering along beside the sheriff was the most terrifying memory he'd seen yet. Memory? He hoped it was all just a memory. He *knew* he'd killed this guy. He'd bashed his skull in with a hammer. The left side of the bus driver's head was caved in, a gory mess of bone, brain matter and coagulated blood. How could it be that this guy was on his feet, lurching towards him with a bloody hammer grasped in his fist?

As the car neared them, the sheriff unclipped the nightstick from his utility belt and drew back his arm to strike. At the same time, the bus driver readied the stained hammer.

Marty wasn't thinking anymore, he wasn't doing anything except cringing in fear. His crossed arms covered his head and he ducked down low. He felt the blows land on his wrist and back, the sharp pain a reminder that this was all too real, and then the car was past them.

He could feel tears running down his face, stinging him as they washed across the cuts and scratches on his cheeks. Aside from the clacking of the car as it raced forward, it had grown silent. With considerable effort, he willed himself to raise his head again.

The blackness that surrounded him was lightening to a dark, swirling, fog-like gray. Up ahead he could just make out several people lining each side of the track. He had flickers of recognition as he sped past them, the eyes of each of them never wavering from him.

There was a middle-aged school teacher he'd roughed up for her purse money. He saw the high school kid he'd jostled passing on the sidewalk and then beaten bloody when the kid flipped him off. There was an old man he'd thrown to the ground next to an ATM unit when the guy made him fight for the cash he'd withdrawn. There was even a guy he'd done a break-in with. After the job, he'd coldcocked the guy with a pipe so he could have all the jewelry they'd stolen for himself.

There were more of them ahead, plenty more, lining each side of the track, just watching him with unblinking eyes. And just as quickly as they had come into view, they were gone. With a gasp of relief, it occurred to him that maybe the worst of it was behind him.

The gray darkness took on a slight greenish hue, and in the dimness he could make out what looked like small blotches. First one, then another, and then another. But as the car drew nearer to them he could see that he was looking at the ends of shafts of wood. They were long, with jagged sharp tips. There were at least a dozen of them now, and they were all pointed at him. The car was bearing down on them with increasing speed, and they were all pointed right at him.

He struggled fiercely, twisting, insane with fear as he tried to dislodge himself from the car. His mouth went dry. He had to free himself.

The wooden spikes were only a few feet away now. The safety bar suddenly released and sprang upward. At the moment he stood up, he realized it was too late. He heard himself scream a loud, empty, lonely scream.

CHAPTER TWENTY-TWO
NOW YOU SEE HIM

L arkin stood at the rear of the building housing the dark ride, shining the beam of his flashlight over the metal maintenance door.

"It only opens from the inside, with one of those emergency release bars, just like the door on the side," Romero said. "He must've jumped out of the car as soon as he was inside and slipped out through one of these doors."

"Not without being spotted by the two other units that pulled up in the parking lot as I followed him over the fence," Larkin responded.

He stepped away from the door and headed back towards the front of the building.

"Those guys went over the fence after I did, not more than a minute behind me," Larkin continued. "They'd have been approaching the rear of the building just after Wedlow went inside."

They made their way around to the front of the building, stepping into the bright blue and red glow from the emergency lights on the six cruisers that had parked in between the various rides in the area. Beyond the cruisers was a city ambulance. Larkin could see the girl sitting on the rear bumper. A detective he recognized, a guy named Marsten, stood next to her.

He turned back towards the dark ride building in time to see two of the officers who had followed him over the fence coming out of the ride's tunnel at the exit side. Two other officers soon appeared from the tunnel on the entrance side.

"Anything?" Larkin asked.

"Nothing but a lot of fake scary shit," an officer answered.

"No sign of him," his partner added.

"Damn it!" Larkin cursed. "He can't have just disappeared into thin air."

"There are plenty of places to hide in there, but I gotta tell you, we covered it good," the officer assured him.

Marsten left the girl with one of the ambulance attendants and joined them.

"How is she?" Larkin asked him.

"Shaken up. She's got a couple of nasty bruises and some minor cuts, but she'll be okay," he responded. "Any sign of your guy?"

"Nothing," Larkin answered.

"What about the ride operator? What's he have to say?"

"No sign of him, either," Romero answered.

"The guy was nowhere to be seen by the time I reached the ride," Larkin explained.

"You weren't kidding when you said Wedlow has a knack of slipping out of tight spots," Romero said.

"Don't rub it in," Larkin grumbled.

"Not me, man. I'm right there with you," Romero assured him.

"Officer Larkin, Detective," a voice called out.

They turned to see a young uniformed officer approaching from the direction of the pier, the beam of his flashlight swaying back and forth in front of him. He looked unsettled and nervous.

"What's up?" Larkin greeted him.

"You better come see this," the officer said, a tremor in his voice.

They all followed the officer back towards the pier.

"So what're you showing us?" Larkin asked, not in the mood for any guessing games.

"You just better see it for yourself, sir."

"Patience is a virtue," Marsten quipped.

As they approached the pier, Larkin could see several uniforms gathered at the guardrail some seventy-five feet out from the pier's entrance. Each of the men were shining their flashlights over the rail at the shoreline below.

None of the men said a word as Larkin, Romero, and Marsten joined them. Larkin leaned over the rail and followed the flashlight beams.

"Shit!" he heard Romero exclaim.

A dozen of the original pilings from the old pier jutted up out of the sand along the shoreline, some reaching above the beach higher than others. The tide water flowed up and around the wooden posts, caressing them with foam for several seconds before withdrawing again.

On a single piling about six feet high, Marty Wedlow, face up and bent backwards, lay impaled. His eyes were open wide in horror, his mouth was frozen open in an ugly, silent scream. The jagged, sharp end of the piling, dark with blood, protruded from Wedlow's chest almost a foot.

"How do we get down there?" Marsten asked.

The young officer who had fetched them pointed back inland. "There's access stairs right there. You can see the opening in the rail.

Less than two minutes later they were standing beside the body. Up close and with the light of four flashlights on the body, the scene was even more horrifying.

"He was bottled up in that ride," Larkin said. "How the hell did he end up here?"

"More to the point, how did he end up like this?" Romero asked.

"He didn't jump," Marsten observed. "I'd say we're at least twenty-five feet from the edge of the pier. He'd have to have wings to make it this far."

Larkin pointed. "He's got some pretty ugly scratches on his face and arms. Whatever did it was sharp enough to shred his shirt."

"Move the lights closer," the detective instructed, stepping closer to the body. "He's got burns, too. His skin's blistered and his clothing's scorched. How the hell did that happen to him?"

They stood in silence, each of them trying to make some sense out of what they were seeing, working to come up with some explanation that might make sense in an official report. Larkin looked up at the pier and then judged the distance back to the body. There was no way

Wedlow had landed here from the deck of the pier. This looked like the guy had dropped from a plane and landed on the piling, or maybe like he'd been thrown down on it with a lot of force. But that was impossible.

"Hey, who's that guy?" one officer asked, nodding his head towards the pier entrance.

They all turned to look.

A tall, dark figure stood at the edge of the pier, staring down at them with black, empty eyes.

"The ride operator," Larkin said.

"Him we need to talk to," Marsten said.

All of them sprinted back towards the access stairs. Larkin kept his eyes on the strange man above them. It didn't surprise him when the strange man unhurriedly withdrew from the pier guardrail, disappearing from sight. As he bolted up the stairs, Larkin felt with a strange, unexplainable certainty that they would never see the ride operator again.

DID YOU LIKE THIS BOOK?

I WOULD APPRECIATE YOUR HELP

Without five-star reviews, independently published books like this one are almost impossible to market.

Leaving a review will only take a minute. It doesn't have to be long or involved, just a sentence or two that tells other readers what you liked about the book. This helps other readers know why they might like it, too.

The truth is that very few readers leave reviews. Please help me by being the exception.

Sincere thanks in advance,
P.G. Kassel

OTHER BOOKS BY P.G. KASSEL

Siphon

A Cayden March Thriller

Black Shadow Moon

Stoker's Dark Secret Book One

A Supernatural Vampire Thriller

Black Hunters' Moon

Stoker's Dark Secret Book Two

A Supernatural Vampire Thriller

ABOUT THE AUTHOR

P.G. Kassel (Phil to his readers) is a former film and television writer-director turned novelist. With over 30 years working in the entertainment industry his teleplays have been produced for television, and his feature length screenplays optioned by major studios and production companies.

He is married to an amazing and beautiful woman who puts up with all his artistic moodiness. They make their home in Los Angeles, California.

If you have any questions or comments for Phil, connect with him online:

phil@pgkassel.com
www.pgkassel.com
https://www.facebook.com/pgkassel

ACKNOWLEDGMENTS

Many thanks to my readers who made the time and effort to help me make this book the best it could be.

Jeanine Carbonaro
Deborah Eyre
Shannon Havard
Judy Johnson
Amanda Jordan-Martin
Arthur Lacey
Brenda Moser
Bob Palermini
Lois Welsh

www.ingramcontent.com/pod-product-compliance
Lightning Source LLC
Chambersburg PA
CBHW021029221025
34378CB00010B/96